It's Not Too Late For Love | Yaffa Feigin-Reich

Producer & International Distributor
eBookPro Publishing
www.ebook-pro.com

It's Not Too Late For Love
Yaffa Feigin-Reich

Translation from the Hebrew by Grace Michaeli

Contact: yaffafay@bezeqint.net
ISBN 9798696901145

IT'S NOT TOO LATE FOR LOVE

YAFFA FEIGIN-REICH

"Many waters cannot quench love
Neither can the floods drown it"
(Song of Songs 8:7)

Ben Gurion Airport

December 21, 2018. I'm sitting at the Aroma café, facing the arrival's gate at the Ben Gurion airport, waiting for him to arrive. Me, an 82-year-old woman, in the throes of an amazing process of love and sexuality, waiting as a disposable cup of fragrant coffee is placed in front of me.

He arrived on the 22 El Al flight from JFK. The flight has already landed. He is going to walk through the entrance gate any minute now, the man whom I refer to as the "Love of My Life."

The Love of My Twilight Years…

Hilton, Tel Aviv

The year, 1975. Sasha Alexander (Alex) Newton non-chalantly leans on his elbows at the corner of the bar at the Tel Aviv Hilton hotel, with a glass of whiskey in hand. A seemingly eternal cigarette hangs naturally from the corner of his chiseled lips. A straight upturned nose, with brown hair and streaks of gold, broad shoulders and narrow hips. He was wearing an unbuttoned cotton shirt, made of a thin powder-blue fabric, exposing a thin patch of hair on his smooth and tanned chest.

He looked like the epitome of "what every woman wants," and diving into his deep-blue eyes, one could get lost in those eyes, peering into the inner gaze, as if drowning in a profound lake, its shade shifting to gray steel according to his mood. The expression wrinkles on his face created a charming and sympathetic smile.

His right brow would curve sharply upward when he

would carelessly blurt the sentence, which had become a cliché: "And whoever leaves this fucking country last should remember to turn off the lights in Lod" (Ben Gurion Airport's former name).

Sasha was one of the famous former USSR aliyah activists who had come to Israel in the 70s. Thanks to his developed business sense, along with his national lectures, Sasha had quickly become one of the leading insurance agents in the country. However, he would always see himself as that same little boy, starving and fleeing for his life in WW-II Russia. That image was imprinted within the depths of his soul and would constantly torment him, like that heavy golden Star of David necklace he never took off, making him look like a crude macho-man. Yet it didn't seem to bother him, as though he wanted to constantly remind himself how much he had succeeded and of the wealth he had gained. He would joke: "let them be jealous."

Thanks to his high rank in the Red Army, Sasha left his army service at the IDF as a lieutenant colonel in the Paratroopers Brigade.

After an exhausting practice at the Hilton's Nautilus spa gym, Shoshana (Shosh) Kineret sat in a comfy armchair in the corner of the hotel lobby. There, between the bar and wide windows overlooking the gardens facing the beach and surfers, she had a hot cup of coffee and carefully examined Alex.

The Good Life

Past events flash before Shosh's eyes:

They'd known each other for two years, at least. He kept taking care of her insurance policy, by force of habit – her car insurance, apartment, personal injury coverage, all of which were a drop in the bucket compared to his business operation. Nowadays, he mostly managed industrial insurance for factories and powerful financial networks.

He would always carry out his business sternly, charging his commission in full, no discounts. He wouldn't offer her any discounts, either, and would add almost apologetically, "I'm sorry, Shosh, but when it comes to business, I'm like a shark. I work according to my own seismograph, no special rates or discounts for friends. But you'll always get premium service."

"Marry me and you wouldn't pay a dime," he'd add

casually, with a smile flickering in his bluish-gray eyes.

"Are you serious?" I asked. "I wouldn't marry a Don Juan."

"I love you, silly. There's no one else."

His company offices stretched over an entire floor in one of the new central Tel Aviv buildings. I would occasionally visit at the end of his workday, when the offices officially closed, where I would find him on his own. When I would arrive, he would immediately brew me a Turkish coffee with cardamom, and its aroma would spread through the room. We chatted as we bit into our crispy schnitzel and fries, wrapped in pita bread with hummus, tahini and salad. He had ordered this lunch earlier from the tower's restaurant. After we finished our negotiation and I signed the necessary documents for the insurance policy renewal, I found myself embraced in his arms, with my head resting on his large and protective shoulder. I loved those moments.

I sat cradled his in arms, listening to his fascinating stories, later me telling him mine. We exchanged some pecks and fond bites of each other's earlobes, necks and chins. We made out as his warm hand caressed my ample bosom, my perky nipples, and kept chatting to prolong the moments before our future pleasure.

From these conversation snippets, I got to know him,

mostly the little boy inside of him, the one he had told me about on one of those days.

In the end, we got married. The wedding was highly covered by the media. Aside from all of my relatives and his friends, it was also attended by the then Prime Minster Golda Meir, head of the opposition Menachem Begin and his wife, Aliza, ministers, Tel Aviv celebrities of the day, academics, paparazzi, and a lot of good friends.

At the beginning of our marriage, we lived a life of lazy leisure. We had breakfast at our Tel Aviv penthouse facing the sea: aromatic, foamy cappuccino with rustic whole-wheat bread slices, smeared with salted butter and plenty of black caviar—received by the kilo from his friends from the former USSR—that we spread with a teaspoon.

We made love whenever we could and, in the evenings I would drive Alex, in our tax-free blue Volvo, to fascinating talks he would volunteer to give in different kibbutzim and other places to which he had been invited.

We loved each other a lot. We were crazily attracted to each other. Our life was good and our sex even better. At times, I would experience multiple orgasms, which would blow my mind, such divine sensation. What I truly never understood was why he'd ask me to take off my own underwear, even when he was insanely horny. Since we regularly went at it at least five times a day, I would walk around without underwear. I wore a simple floral robe with buttons, and he would occasionally approach me completely naked and horny in the kitchen, while I was cooking. He would then unbutton my short robe, grab my naked body and press me to him. Finally, we would find ourselves on the kitchen floor, dripping with sweat and desire, unaware that the food was about to burn. Only the smell of scorched pots brought us back to reality.

Naturally, this didn't last throughout our entire marriage. Later on, it slightly dwindled, but the love was always there, even during crises. We had a charming and domineering daughter that we named Galit, but we fondly called her Gali. Alex's business prospered; we would often travel abroad or go on vacations in Eilat and the Dead Sea. I managed to work and study, completing my master's in political sciences. He kept working, lecturing and writing articles for the press. We kept having sex almost every day.

He was a heavy smoker, which finally left its mark on his health, but we still shared the same love through the years. Love was the operative word, we would collect love, like collecting mushrooms after the rain, like two surfers chasing the high tide in a stormy sea.

Toward the end, we no longer had full intercourse. We would hug, caress each other, and share each other's company until the end—until his health deteriorated. Alex passed away February 1, 2016. I miss him so.

Alex went through a crisis the last months of his life; he would no longer leave the house. He would spend most of his time in the armchair or bed and suffered from bedsores. His memory faded too, the sharp look in his blue eyes had turned dull, but I could still feel all the emotion in them. A caregiver would come to bathe him, and we ordered a special bed for him to ease his pain. I sat beside him in his last moments and spoke to him as I held his warm hand. I felt how, little by little, life was running out of him.

Mr. Weiss' Blessings

The years of WWII... I was reminded of the childhood stories Alex would tell me.

At twelve, I barely remembered what my parents looked like. My memory of them gradually faded and the image of their face waned daily.

I lost my parents during the war, in a crowd at the train station. We waited, like every day at that forsaken station in rural Russia, for a train that was late. It was a cold and dark afternoon. Hundreds of people stood together by the tracks. There were forests behind us. I occasionally snoozed.

I was awakened by a noise, as if the tracks shook. Suddenly, the train everyone was expecting entered the station. My parents, holding my hands on both sides, were swept away by the human wave that pushed them from behind and flowed onto the train. At a certain point, the hands that held onto me were ripped away and I no longer held them. Later, after the war, I found my parents in Israel.

I remember a never-ending cry of agony. It was my mother's voice. I was taken by the masses deep into the train. I kept my head as high as possible above the human wave that washed me away. Mostly, I tried not to fall. On the ground I would have been stomped to death by terrified legs.

The muffled sounds of cannons firing slowly grew closer. The train shook and began moving down the track, steadily rocking until finally rolling off in a frenzy toward an unknown destination.

The cars were packed. Someone grabbed my hand. I recognized Mr. Weiss, our neighbor from across the hall. He was a big-boned and kind man, with a serious countenance. A religious and traditional Jew. He was wearing a brimmed hat and reading Psalms verses. He asked me to repeat the words he said when he handed me a dry piece of bread smeared with a bland spread and a dried-up slice of lekach cake.

"You need to say your blessing before you eat bread," he said.

I suspiciously inspected the people surrounding us.

"Don't fear, little one. We're among friends."

I repeated the Hamotzi prayer: 'Blessed are You, Lord our God, King of the Universe, Who brings forth bread from the earth.'

"Where are your parents?"

"I lost them at the train station, Mr. Weiss."

"Are they on the train?"

"No, they stayed outside."

"You'll find them someday," he said.

"Poor child," Mr. Weiss whispered to himself.

It was the last train. I can't remember how long the ride was. All I remember was constantly dozing off. I prayed with Mr. Weiss every time I ate bread and cakes. After we ate, Mr. Weiss insisted that we say grace, the *bentshn* (from Yiddish⬛). The prayer had beautiful and familiar songs that reminded me of my father's home. He would say grace after meals with the words 'next year in Jerusalem.' After the prayer he would tell me of that land, a land of milk and honey, where every Jew can live.

I always thought that people travel to the Land of Israel to die there. The elderly people who would visit my grandfather, may he rest in peace, would always say that a good Jew should be buried in Jerusalem, at the Mount of Olives. This was not the time to dream of Jerusalem, but rather of my next meal.

***

"I met Mr. Weiss in Israel, many years later," Alex continued to tell me his story.

"Alex, didn't we meet at Mr. Weiss'?"

"That's right, do you remember?"

"Of course, isn't he the farmer from the Jordan Rift Valley? We both went to his first grandson's bris; that's where we met."

I remembered a long table covered with a white tablecloth. In the middle of the table was a massive, tall silver candelabrum with seven arms.

The baby was picked up from its stroller and placed on a silver platter, its rim padded with a silk lace blanket. The women took off their bracelets and golden necklaces and covered the silk blanket that wrapped the newborn, who was placed like a prince, laying among the diamond-encased jewels. The "Ali Baba" treasure that gleamed against the silk and lace was intended to bless the crown prince with wealth. After the jewels were returned to their owners - fair women in their finest clothes, sturdy farmer women, some of them rich – the baby was given to the grandfather, Mr. Weiss, who beamed with joy.

The mohel, who would perform the bris, received

the baby from the grandfather's hands. The bright, silk and lace blanket was pulled aside. A cute powder-blue woolen pant, which had been lovingly knitted, was carefully removed. Under the white diaper was the pink skin and tiny genitals of an eight-day-old baby. The baby, awoken by the touch of the hand, smiled indifferently to the mohel. A bit of sweet wine was poured from an ornamental silver goblet onto the baby's lips, which blossomed open like a flower.

And then everything happened in a flash.

He said a prayer. The mohel pulled the foreskin at the tip of the newborn's penis and snipped it with traditional stainless-steel scissors used specially for circumcisions.

I remember seeing antique bris scissors with Hebrew writing on them in an antique store. They were round and silver, with butterfly shaped wings, and two crisscross blades for marking, closing and cutting the foreskin.

The baby started crying rhythmically and slowly. When the baby's wails began, "Mazal Tov!" and other greetings rang through the hall.

"You look sad," I heard a voice behind me. I turned around. It was Sasha Alex Newton.

"No need to be sad, they snip off the tip and it grows back. I promise you that the baby doesn't suffer."

"If that's true, then why does he cry?"

And then he reacted in a way that was characteristic of when he had had too much to drink: "He cries because he just found out he was Jewish." This was when I had discovered Alex's talent for telling jokes so old that they had their own beard, especially jokes about Jews.

He smiled an irresistible boyish smile. He was dressed in yuppie-elegant style, with a leather belt and sandals; he reminded me of a walking fashion magazine.

I imagined him making house visits to bored and horny housewives whose husbands were at work and their children at school or daycare. I straightforwardly told him that.

"And what's wrong with that? Can't I have both business and pleasure? Usually it's the women who initiate. I'm as decent as a boy scout, sitting quietly, it's them who call… besides, these days I work with factories and corporations, I don't do house visits anymore." And this was where he thought it appropriate to add, "But when I want something, I'm like a bulldog. I never let go of my pray!"

At that moment, I couldn't have known how true that was.

Then he remarked, "I'm afraid, my dear Shosh, that I made a quite a pitiful impression on you that day…"

Alex Meets Igor

I return to Alex's story, sometimes I refer to him as Sasha and at times Alex.

I can't remember how I managed to lose Mr. Weiss, too. When we got off the train, people started running. This time, I really fell down. I was trampled over. I fainted. Someone picked me up. I remember a man covered in mud, and then a truck. I recall a long walk through a thick forest. The man whose face was covered in mud tended to me. I don't think I would recognize him today if I were to see him again, but I would know his voice. The mud clung to his face, hair, his eyebrows and lashes. Later, I realized he was injured, too. People in the forest helped us. They were partisans. I stayed with them for a couple of days. Later, after we'd wandered the forest for hours, they told me that we needed to part. 'The forest ends here, and we have tasks to complete.' They tied a folded handkerchief around my neck, and in it they placed baked potatoes. They gave me a canteen and showed me the way I should head. I can't remember how long I walked. Suddenly, I found myself on a street. Where was I? A man dressed in an army uniform approached me and said it was Moscow. But I shouldn't stay. I must leave the city. He kept walking toward the rural areas, leaving the city as I, on the other hand, was swallowed by it.

The streets were abandoned and so were the houses. Rare and faint lights flickered from oil lamps, flashed here and there as evening fell. I noticed a boy walking toward me. He looked two years older, filthy and dressed in rags. I was dusty and dirty too, and probably looked like him. He gestured with his hand. I approached him.

"Come quick," he said, "we need to hide." He pulled me along.

"Why? The Germans haven't arrived," I replied.

"No, the Germans haven't arrived, nor will they. Come!" he said, "little boys shouldn't wander alone at night. No one must know where a little boy goes to sleep."

"Why?"

"There's great famine in Moscow for the past few months. Some people will eat anything."

"Even dogs and cats?"

"Dogs and cats, that's a good one! We don't have those kind of animals anymore. Even rats are scarcely found. I'd love to find one…"

I didn't know whether he was joking or trying to scare me. He wasn't joking. He was dead serious. His look was cold and distant. His expression seemed frozen. Beneath his sealed expression, I could see a friendly smile stretch across his lips. There was something pleasant about him, too. He had black locks that covered his forehead. This wasn't a boy I was speaking to, or an adult. I realized in that very moment that my childhood had faded away, vanished and gone. I was no longer a boy and I may never see my parents or Mr. Weiss again, and I couldn't cry anymore. I was not yet an adolescent, because I hadn't had my Bar Mitzvah, but I wasn't a man either. I had suddenly lost my childhood, like a girl losing her virginity.

He pulled me after him into a ruin, near a crossroad, from which we could look outside and control all entrances. The house was abandoned, and he had prepared a hiding place beforehand, in case someone should surprise us.

"Stick to staying in ruins, no one comes here," he said. "Sometimes, in the undamaged houses, you can see shadows moving. They're people or ghosts. You better be careful."

"Are you scared of ghosts?"

"No, I don't fear the dead. I fear the living."

As we sat in our hiding spot, I took off my handkerchief and opened it. There were two potatoes in it.

"Here, have one," I offered him.

"No," he replied. "We should keep one for tomorrow, let's share one."

"What's your name?" I asked as I split the potato in half.

"Igor."

"And my name is Sasha, or Alex. But, hey, Igor, how did you manage to last this long?"

"At the beginning, I went through all the empty houses and took anything edible. Dry bread, biscuits, fruits, onions, potatoes. I had quite the stock. Then, my friend and I would catch fat mice..."

I didn't actually believe his mice story. But I didn't want to dispute it either, because it seemed to me there weren't any mice left in Moscow. There was nothing left to eat there, and the mice had long migrated.

The next day, Igor taught me something that helped us survive for some time.

"Let me show you something, but you'll have to come with me."

We left the next day early in the morning. The sun shone and sent cool rays. After we passed by a couple of empty streets, we reached a square that looked like the center of a neighborhood in town.

"Can you see the good women standing in the square?" Igor asked me. "They come here to purchase food. Take my word for it, they always come back with something to chew on."

"How do you know?"

"Sasha, you should know, these meaty Russian women know how to handle themselves. They always have someone to feed at home, a child or a husband in hiding, or perhaps an elderly father. They're like lionesses protecting their cubs. You should remember that, in prides, the lionesses are the hunters."

"But even if you do find something, how would you convince them to let go of their prey?" I thought he was joking, but his expression remained serious. "Take a good look," I added, "they walk around with empty hands, without any bags. If they're buying food for a small child, you wouldn't steal the meal of another, would you?"

"No, Sasha. Survival is crucial. In a couple of hours, you'll agree with me. Now, come, they're handing out bread."

A soldier was handing out slices of rustic bread from a military truck.

I managed to get a piece that wasn't too dry. Igor instantly shoved the slice into his shirt, but I was so hungry that I began eating.

"Don't you dare do that!" Igor roared at me. I couldn't understand what he meant. But when I took a bite of my bread for the second time, I felt a strong tug. I thought that my mouth and teeth were being ripped away. I turned around and all I could see was a small shadow, running away with my bread.

Igor burst out laughing. "Now do you get it?" he remarked sarcastically.

"Lesson one complete," Igor said.

"Let's start our second lesson. See, Sasha, these good women don't hide the food in their bags. They hide it in their bosom, deep in their cleavage."

"But Igor, you hide your slice in your shirt, too."

"That's right. They have other hiding places, in the hems of their coats, in special concealed pockets sewn into their dresses. You wouldn't believe what clever hiding spots they find."

"Okay, then, off to work," Igor concluded. "The hiding place you should care about most is the one that can be easily reached and lets you run away as fast as possible.

That place is their cleavage of course, their bosom. There, between their breasts, you'll always find something; a slice of bread, a sausage wrapped in a newspaper, an apple, and even lumps of beef wrapped in fabric.

"Now, you might wonder, what's your next step? Well, first, choose your prey. Preferably someone who isn't too tall. You first make sure that she's on her own, without any friends. Then you start following her. It's best to choose your victim in the crowd and then you can disappear without taking any risks."

"Listen, Igor. You talk too much. You're making it sound like science. What do I do when I'm next to her?"

"You approach quietly and steadily, without her suspecting a thing. You tell her that she dropped something. Usually she bends over to check. Then you act. You quickly shove your hand into her cleavage and pull out whatever you find inside and run away. Sometimes it can even be amusing, you can burst out laughing from the face they make when that happens to them. One of them actually let me caress her breast."

"Oh, Igor, I don't care about breasts."

Igor and his stories. Nonetheless, I was still a child. I still hadn't had my Bar Mitzvah, but I was twelve and a half and sometimes at nights I would wake up wet, and it wasn't because I had peed myself. I looked older than I was. At times, I would enthuse at the sight of my penis, it seemed huge, and frankly, I *was* interested in breasts, sometimes I could think of nothing else. But shoving my hands down a strange woman's chest, I shuddered at the thought. But if she has a sausage or ham down there, I wouldn't be able to resist.

I struggled to believe that things happened like Igor described them.

"Didn't you have any qualms, Alex? These women were looking for food for their children or sick husbands and you took it away from them?"

"No, no, I didn't steal, Shosh, I was trying to survive. Besides, I never took it all, I would take some and leave them a fair share. "Shosh, you cannot imagine the scent of real poverty, the smell of lack, the sour scent of human insult. Death followed us everywhere, every step we took. We lived from one day to the next. It was either eat or die. And every day that passed, symbolized the victory of the little boy I was. Igor, who was older than me, acted on the outside as if it were all a joke, but he was crying on the inside. The pain was too hard to bear. In the world back then, there were only strong people and weak ones. No middle ground. These women, Shosh, they knew how to handle themselves, they were strong women, ballsy women."

One day, as I had my daily route with Igor and my hand was buried deep into some woman's bosom, the plump young woman grabbed my hand tightly.

I was anxious and began shaking like a leaf.

She turned her head to me, her blue eyes shooting lighting. Suddenly, she burst out laughing, as she inspected me from head to toe. My hand was still deep in her bosom, seized in her hand. She took my hand and placed it on her soft breast.

I was scared, but I didn't try to run away. I stayed put, as though paralyzed. Although I had sexual urges, I didn't know what to do about them. This new sensation wasn't unpleasant.

She was about 19 years old, or twenty, perhaps even older. At first, she seemed scary and mean. She was relatively short, compact and strong, her eyes were cornflower blue, her hair was luscious and blonde, and her breasts were like a wide balcony. I was suddenly very warm; I began to blush.

Out of the corner of my eye, I noticed a smiling Igor.

She wasn't in a rush. She realized I was a virgin. Suddenly, she pulled me gently to the nearby yard. She walked hunched, with my hand still tightly pressed into her bosom. She was stout, making us both almost the same height, as I staggered behind her.

Today, this story may sound slightly pedophilic, a little boy with an older woman. But those were days of war. These women's men were at the warfront, captive or in hiding, and no one really cared. The warmth and embrace of a woman was enough compensation for me, for the childhood I had lost. I was neither a boy, nor a youth, nor a man.

We stopped in a dark yard. She stood in front of me, gently pushed me against the brick wall surrounding the yard. I still couldn't decide whether it was for better or for worse. Whether I would receive a caressing touch or a blow for what I had done. Physically, she was much stronger than me. I was a scrawny boy back then.

All of the sudden, I had the urge to gaze at her breasts.

"Don't be afraid!" she said, as she unlaced the strings of her bra. She took both of my hands and placed them on her breasts. "Here, cup them with your hands and caress them roughly. You can suck the nipples, too."

Her nipples burned under the touch of my hands. I thought I was going to lose my mind. All this softness surrounding me. It had been a long time since I had enjoyed a treat.

My knees trembled, but then, I don't quite know how, I regained my senses. For the first time in my life I was thoroughly aroused, hoping for a caring hand and some love. I began to take initiative. I thrusted my head between her ample boom and caressed them passionately, yet gently. I kissed them and then began to suckle on each of them. First one and then the other. Neither of us was in a hurry. We had all the time in the world. She encouraged and guided me. I grabbed her thick and meaty arms, and pressed myself into her soft, pleasant flesh. It was obvious to me what I was looking for; I was looking for a mother, or a woman, a girl. I was so eager for some warmth, fearing what I had done, yet, intoxicated by the wonderful feeling of titillation that had enveloped me, one I had never known. I was also pleased with the fact that she hadn't pressured me and allowed me to take my time. In her heart she knew that this was my first time and that I was still a boy.

I caressed her breasts for quite some time, at my own pace. I forgot time and space. I bit her lightly several times. She seemed to like it. She moved her body in rhythmic circles, answering some deeper question as she determinedly pressed me against the wall, as if trying to push me through it, squeezing me against her and it. I felt my engorged penis about to explode. I noticed her thrusting her hand into her underwear and touching herself. She heaved. With a moist hand, she unbuttoned my shirt and began kissing my neck, my ears and my breastbone. My pants were tied with a rope. Belts were a rare commodity in those days. She undid the rope and exposed my dick, gasping on sight. She cupped my balls with her hands and then lowered her head and began to lick my dick and put it in her mouth. Though I was young, sometimes at night I would get an erection. Her kisses and stroking made my body stretch. Her tongue moved up and down my thick and erect penis. The feeling was amazing, I was insanely aroused. I didn't want to climax just yet, though I felt I was about to burst. I lifted her to me, again drawn to her warm breasts that I kissed in a sensual haze.

I stood on a wide stone there in the yard, now at her height. The blood pulsed through my temples. The tip of her breast was firm and full. She pulled my hand into her underwear. It was all wet and moist in there. Her thin pubic hairs were so warmly wet. Her skin was hot. My body was attentive to her touch, I felt that my penis was fully erect, penetrating its way between her legs, she guided me with her hand. I probably touched her clitoris. Her body was shaking. It was now that I stood steadily on my feet and felt that my erection was that of an older boy. She grasped me, and momentarily slipped her finger into my behind, supporting and lifting me to her belly with sturdy arms. I felt myself inside of her. I started moving like a madman, squeezing her breasts and suckling yearningly. Her breath was heavy. I moved inside of her, encouraged by the rhythm of her body that synchronized with mine. She began to call out loudly, with a crazed moan. My member was entirely wet, as if washed by the ocean, slipping inside of her, no longer fearful, liberated and with increasing gratification. She still held on to my buttocks, the wet tunnel inside of her vibrating in waves, rubbing against my large erect penis. For the first time in a woman I felt my sperm erupt and flow like fireworks, both of us roaring like lions at the climax of our carnal celebration.

I was shocked by Alex's graphic description. My Alex, hopelessly horny.

"Shosh, don't be mad. It was my first sexual experience. Believe me my darling, despite the conditions under which it happened, I still dream about it, and about her as I dream of you. I, Sasha Alex Newton, a small, hungry, mid-war boy, satisfied a real woman. To this day, when I'm reminded of it, I know it was one of the best fucks of my life. She helped me tie my pants and arranged my shirt. Revealing a secret pocket in her coat, she filled my shirt with ham, dry fish, bread and two apples. It was enough for a real feast. That night, Igor and I ate well. We never returned to the square.

Outside, there were different rumors and we didn't want to put ourselves at risk again. We heard from a mutual friend that she would arrive there and even looked for me.

A lot of water has flowed through the rivers since then, there in Moscow's Volga, and here in the Jordan. So many adventures, and plenty of poverty and hardship.

One day we arrived at a farm. We were welcomed by two female villagers, sisters who ran a household on their own. Their men had been in the army for several months. On our way, we'd joined up with a twenty-year-old man, Menachem Mendel. They bathed us and gave us warm clothes, even though it was summer. They made us some potato soup with roots cooked in milk and cream. It was the best soup I had eaten in years. We were tired. They gave us a wide bed and after having finished their cleaning, they came to sleep by our sides. We were sleeping so deeply that we didn't know what was happening. We lay like two zombies as they reveled in our bodies, caressing us, licking and lying on top of us. We woke up feeling elated and entirely wet.

Menachem Mendel woke up early. He had slept on the kitchen bench. He hungrily ate from the soup in the pot and went out to the yard. From afar, he noticed one of the sisters working in the potato field. Menachem Mendel tightened the rope around his pants. The woman was hunched over the ground and was pulling the green stalks, until she successfully yanked out the potatoes. Suddenly, Menachem Mendel noticed that she had lifted her dress to urinate. "Wow," he thought to himself, "she isn't wearing any underwear." He approached her in the field, untied the rope holding his pants, and caressed her buttocks as she went on, yet not pushing him away. He bent over her, found the opening of her vagina and thrust himself in. He sensed the canal gaping inside of her like a magnet, as she swayed her plump behind from side to side and kept pulling up the potato stalks from the ground during their intercourse.

Menachem Mendel, full of the delicious soup, and pleased he had fulfilled his sexual needs, tied his pants with the rope and tightened it. "Now I can join the Red Army," he yelled with joy.

"We can't stay here, we have to move to Leningrad," Igor told me.

By the way, Igor knew I was Jewish. He didn't want to talk about it. Igor's mother was Jewish and so was his father. He was familiar with Jewish customs, but their family didn't keep any of them.

One day, we found refuge in a military supply truck heading north. The driver and the soldier sitting by his side turned a blind eye as we hopped into the back of the truck. In the end, they shared some of their food with us and dropped us off close to our destination. I don't know how we managed to get to Leningrad, but it turned out that things there were even worse. Menachem Mendel stayed with the soldier so he could join the army.

Igor met a group of Jews planning to cross the border to Sweden.

I finally succeeded in joining the Red Army, where I excelled. Before we departed, Igor said to me: "Alex, you are my best friend. If we ever get out of this, you and I, we should meet again.

"But how, Igor? You know I'll eventually go to Jerusalem to try to find my parents, and you'll stay in Russia. How would we ever meet?"

"Alex, I'm not so sure I'll stay in Russia, nor will I come to Jerusalem. If I ever leave, it will be to the United States of America. When is your birthday, Alex?"

"It's easy to remember, August first."

"Listen, Alex. We'll meet when fate allows it, in a year or two, or maybe in ten. If I can, I'll arrive every first of August, at one in the afternoon, to the Red Square in Moscow, where we sat. One day, you might be there!"

"Well, Alex, did you really meet your friend Igor?"

Alex looked down with embarrassment and smiled mysteriously…

I was surprised.

Igor

March 2018. It is more than two years since I was widowed. I was in a crisis after having lost Alex. I kept in touch with several of Alex's friends, and with one of them especially; his best friend, Samuel (Sam), who is now around 80 and who lived with his wife in the Dominican Republic. I corresponded with him by email. He and his wife were visiting Israel for their son's wedding. I kept telling Sam that I missed Alex terribly. Sam told me "Alex and I had a mutual friend who was widowed about a year ago and lives in New York. Alex always wanted to meet him. He's about to visit Israel this April."

I asked him about this friend's name and occupation.

Sam told me he was a doctor. A world-renowned cardiologist whose American name was Mike (Michael) Ziv, but Alex knew him by "Igor."

For a moment, I was horrified - *Igor*?

A Phone Call from New York

"Sam, wasn't that the name of Alex's friend from the war? Did they eventually meet?"

"I don't know. He always cherished Alex. Maybe you can give me your phone number and I'll pass it along to Mike (Igor)."

I told him I'd write him my phone number that very day, and so I did.

For my convenience and due to my difficulty walking and balancing myself, I took my walker that had a seat on wheels. I went shopping and then to the French Embassy to issue a Life Certificate, as I do every year, in order to receive a little stipend for my work in France. While I was there, I also asked to renew my French passport.

The older clerk sitting in front of me remarked: "Why bother having your passport renewed? It's not like you're going to travel anywhere," she concluded.

"Right," I said sadly. Why bother? Then, I regained my composure; why wouldn't I travel anywhere? I was an old woman who needs a cane or a walker to get around. But was that it? Was my life over? I asked her to write down what I needed to prepare in order to renew my passport. They asked for quite a lot of documents, mine and my late mother's consular report, two different passport pictures, one of them with the ears showing.

In short, I left rather disappointed.

I was classified as an old 80-year-old woman whose life was over.

I lifted my head, straightened my back, smiled slyly. "I'll show them all, I'll prove them wrong, me as well."

I hailed a taxi on the main street and asked him to take me to my local café. I ordered a cappuccino with extra foam and four pastries, including small croissants. I did two newspaper crosswords and then walked to the pharmacy. It was 4 PM. I browsed through the aisles. Suddenly, my phone rang. I saw a foreign number with the country code for the United States: +1. My excitement quickly wore off as I saw the 718-area code for Brooklyn or Queens, and not 212 for Manhattan.

I picked up. On the other end, I heard a deep, manly

voice, rugged yet pleasant at the same time. His voice caressed my ears.

"Am I speaking with Shosh, my friend Alex's wife?" he asked.

I replied in a somewhat hesitant and childish voice, "Yes, this is she."

I sat on the walker's seat. Blushed and excited.

"I received your number from Sam. I'll be visiting Israel this April and will arrive mid-month. I would like to meet you. I would like us to visit Alex's grave. I have also lost my beloved wife, Sonya, a year ago."

"I am sorry," I said.

He promised he would contact me once he arrived.

I don't know why I was excited by this conversation. First, since Alex wanted to meet him so badly; they may have met or perhaps life's course prevented them from doing so. But there was something else, Mike's voice sounded like someone's who had always been here. On the other hand, visiting the cemetery was hard for me, because of an incident that had happened when I visited my late father's grave. He's buried at the Haifa main cemetery, facing the Carmel Coast.

A Tale of a Bag of Cucumbers

I remember driving to Haifa to my late mother's apartment, the one paid for with key money and containing different items she would never throw out. I found some of my childhood wardrobe, my Bat Mitzvah dress and so on; I had to sort through them and throw things out. My mom had kept it all. There were records from the beginning of the century, books, and Reader's Digest magazines. The closet was filled with different objects. I remember driving back and forth from Tel Aviv to Haifa, at least 16 times until I cleared out every last item, an entire life thrown to the trash – except for the records.

On that last day we cleared the apartment, I decided that on my way back to Tel Aviv I would stop by the cemetery, which was on the way, and visit my late father's grave, and if I had any time left, I would also visit my mother's, which was just over the hill. My religious cousin had taught me the rituals one should perform when visiting their loved one's grave. How we should go in one way and then leave from another, rinse our hands after the visit in a faucet, and when standing in front of the grave, place a stone and be at one with our loved ones by reading Psalms verses which begin with the deceased's initials.

My late father was buried at the end of the main row. I stood in front of the grave with mixed feelings. I chose the prettiest stone around and stood in front of the grave of my beloved father, at one with his memory. From the corner of my eye, at a close distance, not too far from the grave, I could notice an old, slightly hunched man, wearing a hat and holding a plastic bag in his hand. I started reading the Psalms verses, concentrating in front of my father's tombstone, different thoughts and childhood memories crossing my mind as I read. There was no one in the cemetery save that man. The sun began to set and glistened upon the waves. A nice breeze blew over my face. Suddenly, I felt someone touching my right shoulder. I kept standing in my place in front of my father's grave, reading the verses from the little Psalms book. I didn't respond.

Once again, I had felt the finger touching my bare shoulder. This time, I turned around. The hat-wearing old man stood next to me and pulled a huge cucumber out of the plastic bag in his hand. He handed me the cucumber and said I should eat it in front of the grave. We were on our own, there was not a living soul. Only the sea breeze disheveled my hair, blowing in the wind. A cowering old man who did not seem at all threatening, holding a plastic bag of cucumbers, demanded I eat the cucumber.

I took the cucumber. I rather dislike them, aside from those I have chopped thinly in salads. I haven't heard of any custom of eating cucumbers in a cemetery while facing a grave. He kept pleading to me, distracting me from immersing in the memory of my diseased father. I started biting the vegetable, he stood and stared at me.

Suddenly, I was startled. What was I doing here? I'm no scared little child. I quickly turned around and ran for my life, still holding the cucumber of doom. I didn't want to throw it next to the grave. I reached a faucet, washed my hands. I dumped the cucumber and confidently approached my tax-free, blue Volvo parked by the entrance.

Ever since that incident, which I cannot decipher to this day, I haven't visited a cemetery. Except once, when I had escorted my beloved Aunt Gita, my father's sister, who was a religious, angel-like 90-year-old woman. She wanted to visit a couple of graves, including that of her late husband, and my father's, her brother. When we reached the graveyard, I was surprised to see that she was holding a long list that also had the names of her deceased friends. They were all buried there, particularly one friend, whose full name I will not disclose, though I will say her name is Ruth. She was a good friend of my aunt and they both volunteered at the Chevra Kadisha, sewing shrouds. During one of their visits to the cemetery, Ruth tripped by an open grave and fell into it, breaking her leg. I remember that the family would occasionally joke about it.

Mike "Mon Amour"

April had come, but Mike didn't call. I thought he was supposed to notify me when he arrived and share his plans. I didn't think I had to wait two weeks to hear from him. It was a bit of a bummer. A week had passed, and then ten days, I looked great and was ready to meet him. In the meantime, I came down with a serious flu. Finally, he called a couple of days before his return to the States. I picked up the phone coughing and stuffy and told him that sadly, we wouldn't be able to meet. I didn't specify why. I thought to myself that he should have scheduled with me on the day of his arrival, that he thought too much of himself and I couldn't be bothered. I was even angry and decided to erase him from my contact list. I stayed home with the flu for two weeks. I wasn't sure he actually called and that I had indeed told him I wouldn't be able to meet him. I had somewhat of a blackout.

I hadn't been in touch with him from April until September 2018.

Finally, I decided to ask him via email if he had even arrived in Israel in April. He replied that he had arrived with several of his family members, that he had called, and I didn't want to meet him, so he didn't insist. I responded that he should have called in advance and set a day. He said I was right.

Around Rosh HaShana, I decided to wish him Happy New Year, without any unnecessary flattery.

Which I did.

He greeted me back. He also wrote that he was eager to meet me and that he had visited his friends' tombstones, one of his deceased friends was a terror crime victim who had been murdered in the territories. He told me that he had hosted a large dinner for 30 members of his family and friends at a seafood restaurant at the Tel Aviv port.

He then told me more about his and Alex's relationship, and asked to hear more about me. He kept telling me that he had lost his beloved wife, Sonya, a year ago, and that they had been married for more than 50 years. Before, when he was 22 years old, he had been married to a woman from Kiev and they had a daughter together. I first asked him to tell me about himself, and then I would tell him more about me.

We became closer since September 2018. I loved corresponding with him. We spoke English.

He told me that after the war, he learned medicine and specialized in cardiology, and that he always had a warm spot in his heart for Israel. He had even learned Hebrew and several Hebrew phrases while in Russia. Finally, he decided to leave for the States. He worked at the Mount Sinai Hospital and had a private practice in New York, too. He did well. At first, he lived in a small apartment in Manhattan, then he moved to a duplex that was part of a penthouse on Park Avenue. He had been volunteering for years and performed free surgeries to those in need. He took part in humanitarian aid in disaster-stricken areas across the world, earthquakes in Asia, in Africa and South America. He had often performed surgeries in Africa on children who were born with heart defects.

His wife, Sonya, a sweet woman who loved her family, wasn't fond of the snobbish and yuppie Manhattan. So he sold his penthouse and moved into an edifice in Brooklyn.

I replied with an email telling him about myself. I told him about my work as a journalist, my stay in Paris, my work at the Liberian Embassy, about my daughter, Galit, and my grandson. He sent me pictures of his family.

I told him that I was in fact an old lady, and I had turned 80. I thought he was younger than me, but I knew for a fact that he was older than my late husband by a year or so. I did know, however, that he was also in his eighties.

Three years since Alex passed away. I hadn't been in a relationship with a man since then, and when Alex died, I thought I wouldn't have another. Even before Alex passed away, I didn't have a full sex life. There were many warm and romantic moments. Hugs and kisses with my wonderful Alex, my love. But I had been almost celibate for a decade.

Mike responded that he looks different than his pictures on his scientific publications and that he wasn't that much older than me.

September passed by and it was soon October 2018. He began calling me every day at 8 AM East Coast time, which was 3 PM in Israel; a seven-hour difference. Sometimes we would Skype.

He sent me pictures of himself, of his sons, his daughter, and grandchildren. I also sent him old pictures of Alex and myself, and recent pictures of my daughter, Galit, and grandchildren.

I could tell by the pictures that he was slightly shorter than me. He had broad shoulders, was stout, well-built, didn't have a gut like most men in his age. I noticed his hands. I adored his hands. His hands were gentle and strong, the hands of a surgeon, like a pianist. He still wore his wedding ring, a wide golden band. And just like Alex had, I could see underneath his shirt, a thin golden Star of David necklace glistening. His eyes were warm and brown with an occasional green sparkle. He still had full and natural hair, black with silver strands, blowing in the wind as it did in his pictures from his youth. I loved listening to his slightly hoarse voice. I was falling in love with him like a schoolgirl. He was the only thing I could think of.

I never imagined something like that would happen to me. I thought I was going to age pleasantly, surrounded by my loving daughter and grandchildren.

I can't say I had a bad life. I still miss Alex very much. There had always been men who were interested in me, but I didn't care. With Mike, it was something different, a certain *je ne sais quoi*.

After my husband had passed away, my health deteriorated. I was hospitalized with pneumonia. After the CT scan, I was unconscious for two weeks and was transferred to the ICU.

My daughter thought it was the end. I struggle to

remember what happened during those days when I was unconscious. I remember traveling a lot, mostly trains and parking lots. I didn't meet relatives who had passed away; I saw plenty of old people, whose hair had gone gray. I didn't speak to anyone, and no one spoke to me. I walked from different parking lots to different cars or was taken on a train. I was constantly moving.

Since Mike had come into my life, I felt rejuvenated. This love had given me so much strength. I felt like I could move mountains. I'm not only referring to the sexual awakening I experienced. I wanted him with every fiber of my being. Sometimes, I would cry with joy. I knew it couldn't happen to every woman my age; meeting someone and falling hopelessly in love with them.

Love made me stronger. It changed me completely. I used to fight with the supermarket cashiers, and now, I was so nice to them. Generally speaking, I was much nicer to people and they were reciprocating. Sometimes, my neighbors would smilingly help me carry my groceries to the third floor, even without me asking. I felt the world was smiling at me and it was all thanks to love. Even if he loved me less, I would always love him... an unconditional love.

Tel Aviv – Manhattan

Mike and I spoke every day. I always spoke to him in different places, once I was sitting in a café, I was once walking down a street. Once I decided I would stay home and be alone with him, revel in the increasing sensation of infatuation.

Just hearing his voice would send shivers down my spine, like an electric shock. I would prepare myself for these conversations. They changed my days completely. We started Skyping where he could see me for who I was. I made sure to wear makeup. My hair was quaffed back. I wore a tight sweater in light blue, which was my favorite color. Though I was wearing a bra, my nipples stood out underneath my sweater. I wore delicate jewelry – a gold necklace with diamond, sometimes I would wear a thicker necklace by Van Cleef Paris, with a diamond and an enamel blue butterfly with golden wings. At times, I would wear an H. Stern necklace with the word "LOVE" (like the one on "Sex and the City"). I threw on a jeans jacket, as if I had just returned from shopping. I pulled down my hair, for a more natural look – I didn't want to appear too meticulous – and I sat in front of the computer.

My lips were slightly perked. I pinched my cheeks, but it was unnecessary – I was blushing with excitement anyway. I was prepared for the conversation. I felt his love for me slowly growing. He told me about the day he had, when he spoke to his son, or went to a Chinese restaurant with his eldest granddaughter. It was a casual conversation, but there was a lot of yearning behind it. He told me about Sonya's illness, and how they had spent two years in the hospital as he nursed her. He said that us meeting each other was an act of God, a match his wife had made up in heaven, and that I was destined for him. Sometimes he would call me "my wife." His words oozed love. I pined for him more and more, and so did he. At the end of the conversation, I was elated with passion for him. I felt both a physical and spiritual yearning. This repeated daily, for a long period of time.

One day, when we hung up after one of our conversations, it was hard for me behave as though business was usual. His voice kept ringing in my ears, as if we hadn't hung up. All this made me ecstatic. I felt loaded. I poured myself a glass of Merlot and sat down in my recliner by the window overlooking the palm tree avenue on my street. An afternoon sun shone. I covered myself with a light blanket and took little sips from my wine. I sensed a wetness in my pussy, an inexplicable stimulation. I placed the glass of wine on a small table by the armchair. Tears of joy started to pour down my cheeks. I put my hand in my underwear and simply masturbated, my fingers fluttering on my pussy. I felt my nipples becoming erect. I breathed heavily. His hoarse voice still echoed through my mind. I replayed words and sentences from our conversation. I was so concentrated on him. I wasn't alone, since he was beside me, as if I had felt the touch of his skin and his amazing hands caressing me. My pussy began to blossom like a flower at the touch of my fingers. My clitoris tightened. I increased the pressure. I finished with a strong and dominant orgasm that shook me, wet with female ejaculation; it had happened to me occasionally. Good thing there was a box of tissues around. I stayed there for a couple of moments, my temples burning as I dripped with climactic passion. I sat there sweating and panting. I thought to myself: 'how hilarious, an 82-year-old masturbating and climaxing with passion for her man.' I began to cry with joy again. What would happen when I meet him face to face? Where would our mutual yearning to be with one another take us? I cried for a long time and wiped my tears. It was a good thing that the glass of wine was beside me. I sipped from the velvety Merlot that filled me with a sensation of satisfaction, that I was living the good life. I imagined that he was next to me, and I was resting my head in the dent of his strong shoulders, feeling his skin. I knew I would love to feel his body pressed against mine. It was a good feeling, though he wasn't physically there with me. There was an ocean between us.

I was inspired by him to write a poem in English, the language in which we communicated. A poem that had stanzas and a rhyming scheme. I didn't know the rules of literary writing, lyrics and meter. The poem flowed out of my mind like a beaming waterfall. Good thing I make sure to have a notebook and pen by my side. If I have an idea, I write it down in my notebooks, sometimes just bullet notes, otherwise I would shortly forget. The poem began to materialize, the sentences came to life. I decided to send him the first draft at night – by the end of his day.

Night in Manhattan

A romantic deep-blue night,
sets on the streets of Manhattan.
Embracing the island's skyscrapers,
with a golden sunset light.

It's so very cold there outside,
And here it's warm inside.
Here I am, in a faraway land,
dreaming of a late love I hadn't planned.

Here Jerusalem glows in gold,
the mighty crown it wears so very bold.
The sun sends warm shiny rays,
On the city's walls since the olden days.

A glimmer of acceptance, there glares,
beyond the fresh palms, green and fair.
And you, a creature full of endless love,
hiding behind the buildings, towering above.

The Mediterranean waves,
wash against ancient shores,

our bodies bare, mine and yours,
my sea, your ocean, our love roars.

When your night, and then mine,
shelter our cities, at the same time,
with a protective light,
our love, your night, my morning, and then again,
we shall pray and say "Amen."

Since we'd been speaking, my English improved by the day. Sometimes, I would even *think* in English when it came to him. I was under his spell. I would speak only about him all day.

My daughter, Galit, was annoyed: "You only think of him. It's like we no longer exist. You never think about us, about your only daughter and grandchildren. You have so much here and all you talk about is 'Mike, Mike.' Enough!"

These moments burdened my joy. Why couldn't she just be happy for me, pleased that I had found love at such an old age? This wasn't a fling. Why the sudden hostility?

It has been three years since I was widowed. I didn't expect that things would unfold this way. Children are supposed to leave their home at some point, spread their wings and live their lives. We can always keep helping them if necessary. The parents, whomever of them is still alive, stay on their own and live their life as they see fit. I realize that she wanted to protect me from harm. While it's true I'm old, my mind is clear and active. Shouldn't Grandma have the right to be a happy woman? And not just with her grandchildren, but as a woman in love with a man?

I always felt that a woman needs a man, not just for sex and his masculinity, but rather as a basic human necessity of female versus male, creating a perfect bond that is based on the principles of creation.

I felt that Galit was interfering with matters that had nothing to do with her, that it was inappropriate and that she had no right to do so. The greater my love grew, the harsher her hostility became. I couldn't quite understand what was happening and why wasn't she happy for me. I had never left her. Only when I was a student and she was a little girl, I would occasionally leave her for several hours with a nanny, which I later learned that she had disliked. She had never forgiven me for that.

Alex, my husband, was always preoccupied with his political affairs and private business. My studies didn't bother him. On the contrary, he was pleased that I had something to do during the day, and at night he would make it up to us under the sheets. It was all smooth sailing.

Mike felt the tension and my daughter's disapproval from afar. I told her that I didn't know what tomorrow would bring. Now I was simply happy, and that was it. I wasn't interested in remarrying for many reasons, some of which were financial. Sometimes, when he called me "my wife" in our conversations, it would make me uncomfortable. While I did want to spend the rest of my life with him, I couldn't predict the way in which this relationship would unfold. Aside from my unconditional love, an insane sexual craving and yearning to be in his arms – I didn't know for a fact what it would mean to live with him. I knew that when he arrived, we'd stay at a five-star hotel, go out to restaurants, walks, concerts and shows. In short, something similar to a honeymoon. But I had no idea what my life by his side in New York would look like. I told my daughter that I have to try and live with him for a month or two before we'd discuss the future. Logic overcame emotion. There's no need to be foolish or lazy. We'll wait and see.

Sometimes doubt would sneak to my heart. My daughter began to behave as if I was neglecting her and my grandchildren. Our lives weren't always peaceful, sometimes we had unresolved issues, even when Alex was still with us. After he died, I thought that I should perhaps go to a retirement home to maintain a shred of independence – play the piano when I wanted, write, paint, listen to loud music and go out.

I was aware of the fact that I was no longer young; I suffered from diseases that were characteristic of my age, such as diabetes, mobility issues and fatigue; I even had a minor heart attack. One day I asked my physician: "Tell me, doctor, am I a sick or healthy woman?"

He replied: "If you feel well and have no complaints – then you are a healthy woman."

When it comes to my age, I was already counting down the days; it was hard for me to make long-term plans, though my love for Mike suddenly gave me so much strength. Still, I couldn't tell in advance how many years I had left. I should address these years as though they are my last. I had a feeling that, barring any special issues, I would keep having intercourse even after I turn ninety. But there were no guarantees, and sex isn't everything in life.

Love, a warm embrace and a feeling of togetherness are irreplaceable. This is the way things are, and I should learn to deal with them. This is what I think. I don't know precisely what he thinks, and I don't want to ask him.

He kept working and participating in different functions related to cardiology. He was a very complex man, and one could definitely say that he was no ordinary man who would be content with drinking tea, sitting in his armchair and walking around the neighborhood block. Occasionally, he would be called to Africa to tend to a newborn with a heart defect, or an adult who was in a life-threatening condition. He had also founded a clinic in Kiev, where he employed a doctor and a team of nurses. Once a year, he would invite some of them to his house for a training course at different American hospitals or call them to come to Africa or some other disaster-stricken area.

Mike told me he was about to arrive to Israel on December 21 this year.

A Strange Dream

Today is Friday, October 26. I dread October, which I have always regarded as a fickle and difficult month, both financially and politically, since the Yom Kippur War broke out that month and bank stocks dropped.

During the early morning hours, after everyone had left, I drank my coffee, ate a sandwich, and fell asleep in my recliner.

I dreamed that I was at the airport and I saw Mike in the distance speaking to someone, with their back turned to me. He seemed pretty short. I knew he was about Alex's height. I, a tall and pretty woman, begin to approach, but the closer I come the smaller he gets. Suddenly, he turns to me and smiles. I notice that he is no taller than my knees.

I don't know what to do: on the one hand, I love him so deeply, but on the other, I am ashamed to walk around with him.

In my experience, I have very lucid dreams, some which have later come true. Was this dream meant to warn me from something I couldn't yet apprehend?

It was hard to decipher the dream. The only interpretation is somewhat of a clue that I would somehow be disappointed; something petty would happen on his part. I don't know what. Perhaps, there were forces trying to bring doubt to my heart and come between us, because everything that was happening was too good to be true.

Igor and I

I waited at Aroma coffee house facing Gate 3. My phone rang. A rugged voice on the line said that someone was waiting for me at the entrance to Gate 2. I had no idea where that was. Did I have to take the elevator? The man who spoke to me was annoyed, and said it was across from Gate 3 and they were waiting for me. I didn't like this unexpected complication. I had told him I would wait at the café.

I sat there, sipped from my coffee and looked around. I asked people. No one could tell me where Gate 2 was. Next to the airport exit, almost in front of where I was sitting, I noticed a man with broad shoulders, surrounded by suitcases and bags, holding a cellphone in his hand. I said to myself: 'it's impossible.' I decided I would approach him and find out. The closer I got, the more the person seemed familiar. I remembered his appearance from our Skype conversations. I noticed his disheveled black hair, with silver streaks. He was slightly shorter than me. His body was stout; no gut or fat. He stood with his back to me and was rummaging in his bag. He had probably been standing there for quite some time. I came closer and touched his shoulder. I was wearing a light beige jacket with a fur collar, and underneath it, a powder-blue sweater. I let my hair down and was utterly excited. He turned to me and a relieved smile spread on his face. Mike collected me into his arms and kissed my lips. His eyes teared up. He embraced me over and over again. I also cried. I forgot our height difference and the dreams I had had. I was in the arms of my man.

We took our things; I dragged the little red Samsonite suitcase as he carried all his bags. We approached the car rental desk. It was already hard for me to walk long distances and I was soon tired.

He spoke a bit of Hebrew and said to me, "Come, I want you strong and healthy." Those are the words that have been etched in my memory.

I sat beside him in our rental car, and we drove to the Dan Panorama Hotel in Tel Aviv. When we arrived, I waited for him at the hotel lobby as he brought the keys to our room. Right after we walked into the room, he through all his luggage onto the floor, and I took off my jacket. I thought we'd sit and talk a little, but he immediately bent over me and embraced me, his hands holding me close to his chest as his fingers caressed my bosom. He took my sweater off.

I sat on the king-sized bed, wearing a marvelous black bra I had bought especially for the occasion. I wanted him to look at me and see the bra against my bright skin, and through its lace, would see my perky nipples. He didn't notice, and with trembling hands he unhooked the bra.

"Shosh," he whispered, "Shosh, my love, I want you so badly."

Before I could say a single word, we were already under the sheets, satisfying our cravings for and lusting after each other. It all happened so fast. We didn't even need lube. His muscular legs wrapped around my body. His hard body sunk into my soft body. His member was wildly erect and he penetrated me aggressively, as if conquering some deserted land. Within a short time, I had a mind-blowing orgasm. He slowed for a while then turned on his back and slipped his body underneath me. He reached for my vagina and touched my clitoris. I was ready for another round. This time, there was no penetration. His fingers played on my clitoris with virtuosity, the touch of a surgeon and a genius.

Soon enough, my body was shaken by the touch of his hand. I climaxed again; this time followed by the female ejaculation I rarely had. In that moment, I cared about nothing else besides what was happening in the lower half of my body. He laid next to me and kissed my lips, pressed me against his warm body and gently caressed my breasts. I was over the moon.

Breakfast at the Dan Hotel

Mike had come for a two-week visit. Our plan was to spend time together, visit his and my friends, attend shows at the Habima Theater and concerts, enjoy a sing-along concert at the Genki Club – and be together. We planned to stay in Tel Aviv for a week, two days in Haifa, three days in Jerusalem, and then back to Tel Aviv, until his flight back to New York.

I bought two tickets for two Habima shows. On Saturday, before the first play, we met my daughter, Galit, and my two grandchildren, Alon and Ilanit, at the Art Café by the theater. To my surprise, their first encounter with Mike went well. Galit ordered a cocktail, somewhat rebelliously. We sat together until the play began. My grandchildren were pleased to meet Mike, who had brought them some presents.

We held hands whenever we could. I loved listening to

his hoarse voice and his stories about his life and work. At night, I would snuggle between his arms, and we celebrated life.

The first week, we stayed at the Dan Panorama Hotel in Tel Aviv. The breakfasts at the hotel were rich and varied. As a principle, I prefer having my breakfasts served to me, rather than having to wander around the dining room with my plate. I hate waiting at the omelet station so that the irritated cook would prepare my omelet just as I liked it. Though I was much nicer to people ever since I had recently fallen in love – probably because I had fallen head over heels – I still managed to fight with the hotel omelet chef. There were so many people waiting at the station. I waited patiently, and when my turn came, I asked for an omelet with herbs and mushrooms, no onion. Suddenly, I noticed he added onions. I asked him to remove the onion. The cook frowned. He was angry and lashed out at me: "I make five hundred omelets a day and you want me to take out the onions!" He smacked the stainless-steel counter with his spatula to emphasize the point he'd made. I was still holding the plate, ready to receive the omelet. I was mad. As they say in French, *la moutarde me monte au nez* – "The mustard had risen to my nose." I returned the plate to its place and left the omelet station and the aggravated cook. I didn't return to that station throughout our entire stay at the hotel. I scooped some scrambled eggs onto my plate, a few different kinds of cheese, vegetables, hummus, tahini, and a fruit bowl. I also made a stop at the bread table, and when I finally reached the table, my plate was entirely full. "Big mistake," I said to myself as I approached, but I could no longer retreat. I saw Mike scanning my plate. "Do you think you can finish all that?" he remarked.

I was surprised by his question. I replied that I would eat what I could. I glanced at his plate; it was much more balanced than mine. It happens, sometimes people get carried away, and eat with their eyes. I felt at a disadvantage, and I didn't like that feeling. He soon apologized. "I just don't like wasting food," he said.

"People who had suffered from hunger in their childhood, can't see food wasted." I nodded. "Those were different times," I said. There was an awkward silence. I lost my appetite. And still, I pleasurably ate some of the meal and had some leftovers on my plate, much to his dismay.

On December 23 we drove to the Yarkon cemetery to visit Alex's grave. I suggested that we take a taxi with a driver whom I had met last time I visited. That place had gone through many changes since the last time I had been there. Almost every last bit of land was now a grave. Aside from the burial buildings, in which people were placed within the walls, the ground had been filled with graves and we could barely walk through the spaces between them. It looked like a "grave supermarket.". If I could, I would move Alex to a different cemetery. However, I had been told that the remains cannot be moved. I don't know whether that's true. When we approached Alex's grave, I got weak in the knees. Mike found a rabbi somewhere. I gave the rabbi a note with the exact location of Alex's grave. I decided I would pull myself together. I regained my composure and walked. Seeing Mike, Igor, bending over Alex's grave, my dear husband of more than 40 years, moved me deeply. I felt the connection and bond they had shared. Mike tried to stay composed, yet his eyes teared up.

Wedding Bells

On December 24 at 5 PM, we were supposed to see the play "My Mika," based on the songs of Yair Rosenblum.

After a romantic and indulgent night together, I asked if we could order room service breakfast. He said he preferred having breakfast in the dining room, and afterward we'd take a walk on the beach. The weather was pleasant. We walked hand in hand, barefoot on the sand as the waves caressed the shore and tickled our feet. A nice breeze blew, but it wasn't too cold. After a few minutes he asked if I knew where the rabbinate was. I knew then that he wanted to marry me. We spoke about it and I loved him very much. I replied that it wasn't very far. He grabbed my hand and said: "Shosh, let's go there, now. I want to get married here, in Israel, before I go back. Perhaps we'll make it to the American Embassy and register."

It was 1 PM. We approached the car parked at the hotel parking. I stepped into the car, buckled my seatbelt and held his soft hand. I felt overwhelmed, and it wasn't excitement. I was nervous. Deep down, I knew he was my man, but it didn't make sense. I felt there was something unusual, but I couldn't put my finger on it. It had been only three days since he arrived and since I had met him in person, Skype-less. I had a different plan in mind. I thought we'd spend time together in Israel. Later, I'd come to New York. We'd be there for a month or two, and then we'd decide what to do; get married or live together. Despite the passionate love I had for him, that had taken over every fiber of my being, I couldn't throw myself into such a relationship without having lived together for a while. This right now – hotels and outings – this was all the honeymoon phase; it wasn't real life.

We reached David HaMelech Boulevard. Mike went to park the car. We entered the rabbinate offices. Mike spoke some Hebrew and asked where we could register to be married. We were told we had to wait for a rabbi, who would arrive in an hour. We sat down and waited. Mike smiled and was reassuring. The nervousness I had felt earlier was gone.

Finally, the rabbi came, a nice Chabad man. I showed the rabbi my husband's death certificate. The rabbi prepared all the necessary papers for opening a file. Mike paid about seven hundred shekels. We decided to come back the next day. We wanted to get married before January 7, which was when Mike was supposed to return to New York. The rabbi said that everything would be fine. We took our time at the rabbinate. It was almost 5 PM.

We reached Habima Theater. Mike went to park the car, and I went to get our preordered tickets. We had to take the elevator to the hall. Despite our delay, we enjoyed Yair Rosenblum's songs. It was a typical Israeli musical, with beautiful songs. Mike was enthused.

We returned to the hotel and then we left for dinner at the Tel Aviv port. We reached the White Pergola restaurant, owned by Israeli-Arabs. There was a typical Christmas atmosphere in the air. Though we hadn't made a reservation, they found us a table. Everything was shiny and festive inside. A life-size Santa figure was placed in the center of the restaurant, as well as a tree entirely covered in twinkling lights and paper chains, creating a festive holiday atmosphere. We sat by a table covered in a white tablecloth and were soon enough served colorful and delicious salads. We had a great time, even though it wasn't a Jewish holiday.

I enjoyed his company. I enjoyed listening to his voice and holding hand. I was pleased and told myself I had nothing to worry about. It was as though I melted in his presence. It was so good to touch him, kiss him. I wanted him so badly. When we were intimate in the morning, at noon or night, I would scream with pleasure and sometimes even had multiple orgasms, which was rather rare. I was sexually charged, and it surprised me. Suddenly, everything was loose. I minded no one. I am an old woman who enjoys sex. I would moan and groan uncontrollably. Mike even remarked that someone might call the police, to which I responded that the hotel staff was prepared for these kinds of situations.

The next day, we returned to the rabbinate. Mike, my Igor, was investigated and requested to prove his Judaism. The rabbi who interviewed him, sat right next to a computer screen and found data about his father, who had lived in Israel and remarried, and data about his mother – both items proving his Judaism. All we had left to do was set the date. The rabbi said we could do it once I complete bridal counseling.

I blushed. I was a bride. I walked into the room and sat in front of the rabbi's wife, who spoke to me kindly and seriously. I contemplated. I was an eighty-two-year-old woman who was about to have bridal counseling. After all, I could set any date I wanted. I no longer had my period and we weren't concerned with having children. I assumed there was no matter of purity, but it was no simple thing, either.

The woman said to me, "You have been with him until now." I wanted to deny it, but I kept silent. She continued, "You have been with him. So, from now on you cannot be with him until the wedding date, a day after you've visited the mikveh." She handed me a small kit that contained a pack of thin pieces of fabric. She explained, "You have to wash well down there, every day. Then wipe it with the napkin in the kit. The pack should last for a few days. On the last day you have to go to the mikveh and immerse your entire body, including your head and hair. The mikveh attendant (*balanit*) will help you. Finally, you'll receive a note verifying you visited the mikveh. You can get married on the day after, and only if you bring the note from the mikveh."

The wedding was set for January 2, 2019. We agreed with the rabbi that the wedding would take place at the synagogue in Kfar Chabad.

I left both elated and nervous. It was December 25.

System Failure

Frankly speaking, the wedding made me very agitated. I felt my body weakening. I couldn't explain what was happening to me. I felt as though my immune system was giving in. I had lost control over my own body.

The next day, I felt an itch down my throat and I developed a cough. That night we didn't have sex, as though we wanted to respect and follow the bridal counselor. We slept in each other's arms most of the night.

On the morning of December 26th, Mike started getting dressed for breakfast. I felt a certain weakness. I told him I didn't feel like walking around the dining room and piling up my own breakfast, maybe it was best that I'd order room service. He wasn't too excited about having breakfast on his own. Eventually, he decided to go to the dining room, but promised he would bring me something. I could have ordered room service, but he didn't like that too much. I actually liked room service in five-star hotels. They had wonderful tuna and fried chicken sandwiches. I was getting to know him. He liked things done the way he wanted them, and he wanted me to follow him.

I felt that my flu was becoming worse and I decided to call a doctor.

A doctor came within the hour, diagnosed me with bronchitis and prescribed medication. He refused to give me antibiotics since he didn't hear any wheezing. If things would get worse, he'd prescribe me some.

Mike returned from the dining room with croissants. I made myself some coffee and tea for him. Then we went, Mike and I, to buy my medication at the nearby pharmacy. After taking my medication, I started feeling better, but instead of staying at the hotel in the evenings and order room service, we went out for dinner every day. The weather was getting colder, the sky was getting gloomier and my condition was deteriorating.

That night, we went to the Genki Club. I had made a reservation. Einat Sarouf performed there every Wednesday. It was a real treat; that woman was an energy bombshell. Despite my flu, I had a great time. We ordered a salad and hummus. Mike didn't have as much fun, even though I thought he'd like it.

The next day, we drove to Haifa and stayed there for two days. While we were there, we met some of his and my friends at a wonderful Druze restaurant.

On December 29, we drove to Jerusalem and spent the evening at the Kangaroo restaurant, with lovely Georgian cuisine. We had to drive through the Maccabi Motzeri square (known as Kikar Hachatulot, The Cats' Square), park and continue on foot. I struggled to walk properly; it rained, and I kept taking breaks. Mike supported me with his arm, caressed and encouraged me. "Shosh, I want you healthy and strong," he said. I remembered that he had already said that to me once. We were invited to celebrate the 60th anniversary of Mike's cousin and his wife. It was wonderful, moving and the food was delicious. Despite their long marriage, Mike's cousin and his wife looked like a young couple.

On December 30, during our stay in Jerusalem, Mike made plans with a couple of friends from Pisgat Ze'ev. The weather was exceptionally stormy. I thought it would be best if I stay at the hotel and Mike would go by himself but he refused. I was pale and wasn't feeling well. I felt I was coming down with pneumonia. I struggled to breathe and every step was hard to take. I was very weak. Mike dropped me off by the mall and drove off to park the car. It was pouring and I was completely drenched. I walked to the entrance of the Pisgat Ze'ev mall.

Suddenly, completely uncontrollably, I began urinating like a horse. Thanks to the pouring rain, no one noticed. Mike arrived. We walked into the mall, and I kept peeing. And like that, entirely wet from head to toe, we went to meet his friends. I pulled out a small Shalimar perfume bottle from my bag and sprayed it all around, at least so it could overpower the urine odor. We met a rather elderly couple, a tall and hunched over man and a small woman wearing a woolen hat. We went up to the top floor. They wanted to go to a restaurant that was similar to McDonald's. To reach it, we had to cross a suspension bridge. I felt that I couldn't walk any longer and I pointed at the closest café. They were disappointed because they wanted to have meat, and the café served nothing but salads and dairy dishes. I didn't understand what was happening to me. We were supposed to go to an amazing New Year's Eve party the next day. I was very agitated. I was supposed to get married on January 2 in Kfar Chabad, and on January 1, at 5 PM, around sunset, I was supposed to go to a mikveh in Tel Aviv. Every move I made required a lot of effort.

When I stepped into the car, and pulled the seatbelt, I lost my breath. Things got better between us only when we got into bed.

How I Missed My Wedding

We were invited to a New Year's Eve party in a villa in Pisgat Ze'ev. Even though, like Christmas, it wasn't a Jewish holiday, New Year's Eve or rather Novy God, was without a doubt an important holiday for former USSR immigrants. I remember that Alex, my husband, wouldn't celebrate New Year's Eve, he'd say "it's not ours." We arrived at a very warm and inviting house. About 20 guests had arrived, each brought a wonderful dish from home or a rich salad. We brought the wine. It was a wonderful and moving night shrouded in an intellectual atmosphere. All the guests were highly educated people and famous researchers. We stayed there overnight in separate rooms in the house basement.

In the morning Mike woke me up, and we embraced warmly. I tried to have light banter with him, but he kept telling me to keep quiet so that we wouldn't wake up our hosts. Our luggage was already packed in the car. We left at dawn back to our hotel in Tel Aviv.

When we were finally at the hotel, I could take a shower and relax. We went for breakfast in the dining room. Then we returned to the room and tried to rest for a while. I took off my clothes and snuggled under the soft blanket on our king-sized bed. Mike hugged me gently and knelt over me. He was kind and soothing. We kissed passionately and he came to me, my sweet man. I was so happy.

The closer 5 PM came the more irritated I got. Mike knew I had to go to the mikveh. It kept raining outside. I made myself some coffee and tea for him. It was 4 PM, but I still hadn't gotten dressed. I was slightly detached. Mike didn't say a word. I prepared the note for the mikveh. I had to be there before evening fell, something to do with the sun setting. He came to me and kissed me, but I didn't say a word. I didn't want to go. However, I knew that if I wouldn't go to the mikveh the wedding wouldn't take place the next day.

My daughter called. "You know, Mom, that if you get married tomorrow, you're stepping into unfamiliar territory and leaving us."

I didn't know what to reply.

"Listen, I'm sick, I'm not feeling very well. I don't

know what's happening to me," I said and hung up.

I leaned back against the tall pillows on my bed, as I lay under my soft blanket. I had a headache, and as time passed, my chest felt tighter and tighter. The rain hit the window pane. 'I'm not going, and I don't care what Mike says or does. I'm too tired to fight with him', I finally decided.

I couldn't quite understand what I was doing. The man I loved deeply was beside me and wanted to build the rest of his life with me, and I was behaving irrationally. After all, he was everything I wanted. Mike smiled at me and caressed my head. We hugged. He was a wonderful lover.

My daughter called again. She said that she had a dream and didn't want to tell me. "What was it about?" I said.

"I don't want to tell," she replied.

"What did you dream about?" I insisted.

"I dreamed that you were away in New York. You were tied to a chair in a basement and your arms were covered in blood."

"Oh, come on, you're exaggerating. That's nonsense."

We agreed to meet on Saturday, January 4, for a dinner at the White Pergola restaurant together with my cousin and her husband. I would make a reservation.

It was after 6 PM and I was still lying in bed. Mike spoke to the rabbi and said that we wouldn't get married the next day and that we need to postpone the wedding.

We had tickets to Leonard Bernstein's opera "Candide," based on Voltaire's book, as part of the Leonard Bernstein Festival. It was cold outside, and my flu was getting worse. I coughed. Mike went to collect our pre-ordered tickets. We had to take the elevator to reach our seats. I sat on a chair and took my ticket. I told Mike that he should go to our seats and I'll come a little later. I stayed in that chair in the lobby until the first intermission. Mike came looking for me. We walked to our seats together.

The second part of the opera was both wonderful and grotesque. I coughed a lot during the show, to the dismay of those sitting around us.

After the concert, Mike went to get the car from the parking lot. I told him I would wait outside, and I sat down on a pile of white cement that also had some garbage leftovers on it. We went to the Brothers seafood restaurant.

Mike realized something was happening to me. I told him that I had to stay at the hotel for a couple of days, without going out to different places, otherwise, I would never recover. "Shosh, I want you healthy and strong,"

Mike said. Those words were like spikes piercing my body.

I then realized that my illness was psychosomatic – it had to do with the stress from the unexpected wedding.

A Tale about a Lobster

Before Mike arrived in Israel, my only daughter insisted that I transfer my apartment to her name. I told her that she would inherit the apartment, in any case, and that I had a will signed by a lawyer. She claimed that things were different now that there was a third party involved, and that if we were to get married and something would happen to me, Mike would also have rights to the apartment. She spoke about it over and over again. I agreed. She spoke to a lawyer and he prepped all the paperwork. I went with her to his office, located in one of those city skyscrapers, so that we could sign the documents. All of that took place one month before Mike arrived.

Deep down, I knew it was a hasty decision on my part, and that if I fought with her at some point in the future – which happened rather often – I might find myself homeless, sleeping on a bench in Rothschild Boulevard in Tel Aviv.

She said I had nothing to worry about, and that wouldn't happen. I told her that we need to add a clause to the contract that would clarify that I will live with her until the end of my days, in this apartment or any other apartment she may move to. She said that was agreed and I shouldn't be concerned.

In fact, I was a rather wealthy woman, but I didn't have enough money to buy another apartment. I have money for trips, outings, restaurants, but not for another apartment.

I arrived with Mike at the White Pergola. My cousin picked up Galit and the children, and they arrived after us. They sat us at a table next to the lobster tank. It was rather pleasant. Mike seemed happy and calm. I felt a little better. We held hands. The waiter approached us carrying a tray filled with salads that adorned the white tablecloth like a colorful Persian carpet. The children enjoyed the variety of salads as well as sitting close to the lobster tank. We browsed through the menu as we ate the appetizers. The waiter arrived, professionally peered over us and took our order. I heard that Galit ordered a whole lobster for herself. It was the most expensive dish on the menu and cost twice as much as other dishes. We ordered gnocchi and salmon, while my cousin and her husband ordered the same.

At first, I didn't notice. I was too preoccupied with Mike and myself. He was pleasant and sent smiles all around. I saw that the waiter approached us with a pair of tongs, he reached for the tank and pulled out a grayish lobster that floundered about. The cook would poach the lobster in scorching water for my daughter. The lobster had a black-grayish shade. When served, it would be bright orange. I could foresee we would have a problem because Mike was supposed to pay for us all. Mike kept smiling, held my hand and made sure that everyone around the table was in good spirits.

The waiter set the lobster on the table on a large platter, along with crackers and picks. I noticed that my daughter was struggling to crack the lobsters shell open to suck out the soft white meat. Apparently there was no clarified butter to go with it, either.

As a mother, I know my daughter and her body language very well. She was wearing a red dress and her ginger curls bounced about, as her beautiful eyes seemed to shoot out sparks. She sipped from her white wine and broke the shell with exaggerated motions. With every hit and bite, it seemed that she was trying to eat me.

That was a declaration of war.

Finally, when the check arrived, Mike suggested we

split it. He was no sucker. My daughter was upset. Her face reddened. Galit didn't want our cousin to pay half the bill, yet the latter paid her share without batting an eye. My daughter was shocked and complained to me about Mike daring to suggest we split the check. I told her I would also pay. I realized that Galit was looking for a fight. In three days, Mike would return to the States and I would return to live with her in our apartment.

My health deteriorated. Mike was supposed to fly back to New York in a couple of days. I packed my things at the hotel. We agreed that Mike would carry my suitcase to the apartment, and I would wait in the car. Then he would drive me to my physician. I preferred not going back to the apartment because of the tension between Galit and I, I even hoped that the doctor would send me to the ER. My daughter, on the other hand, thought that I was coming back home, where she could pick a fight. Galit, however, was quite disappointed. Her punching bag would be elsewhere.

A Tale about an ER

Mike drove me to the clinic. I thought he'd come with me to the doctor, however, he preferred staying in the rented car. He wasn't sure whether he could park there. He was probably afraid of getting a parking ticket. He was supposed to return the car to the airport the next day. I was slightly irritated by the fact that the car seemed to be his top priority.

The weather was pretty stormy. It rained, and the wind blew so strong, that I nearly fell over. I struggled to climb up the clinic stairs. I almost collapsed by the front door. The neighbors helped me hit the entrance button. I walked into the elevator and went up the first floor. I fainted at the entrance of the clinic. I fainted on the armchair. Everyone ran to me and brought me a glass of water.

After the doctor examined me, he announced: "You

have pneumonia." In addition, that morning, my toe had started to swell and hurt terribly. He examined it, too. "In any case, I'm sending you to the hospital," the doctor said.

I was glad. I wasn't going home. I would avoid a confrontation with Galit.

The doctor's secretary volunteered to escort me to the car. I walked slowly by her side, step by step. I barely sat in the car, as the strong wind almost blew the car door out of my hand. I pulled the seatbelt.

Mike looked at me, wondering.

"We're going to the ER," I said.

An Incident at the Hospital

We arrived at the hospital. I told Mike where to pull over. We walked to the ER. The wind blew outside, and it poured. I felt that I couldn't walk any longer, and I sat in a booth by the hospital entrance. I told him I would need a wheelchair. Mike left me there and came back with a wheelchair. I was relieved. He pushed me all the way to the ER door. I noticed he was nervous and concerned. It wasn't easy for him, either. He was eighty-five. I think he was also worried about the car and wondered whether he had indeed parked it properly.

When we reached the ER admission desk, a young man stood beside us. To my surprise, Mike addressed him and asked him to take me to the admission desk, because he had to go. I was astonished that this man, a complete stranger, agreed to do it. Mike pecked me on the lips and said he would call me later and let Galit know I was at the ER. I was too weak to respond, but I found it jarring. I wasn't sure what I thought in that moment, or how I should approach the situation. It was very cold at the ER entrance. After the registration process, the stranger asked if I was okay. I replied that I was, thanked him, and then he left.

I waited to be taken to the ER as I held the papers in my hands. People were bewildered: "Are you by yourself?"

Yes, I was alone. I thought that Mike should have been with me and gone through the entire process with the woman who was his future wife, made sure I was treated as well as possible. Instead, he left me there on my own, worrying he'd get a parking ticket.

Later, I thought that if this would have happened to any other woman, she would have left him, regardless of his virtues. Yes, as I previously mentioned, I was very weak, and wasn't thinking clearly.

After a couple of hours, Mike called to ask how I was doing. Eventually, I spent nearly two days in the ER before I was transferred to a ward. Due to the weather, and the busy ER, things went by sluggishly. We didn't receive any food, either. During my first night at the ER, I was moved to a different place. I also didn't receive any food or water in the morning. Then I noticed that someone had stolen the ring Mike had bought me before we registered at the rabbinate. I thought it was a bad omen. I would have to buy an identical ring before I flew to New York. I contemplated. Why was I even thinking about it in light of his behavior at the hospital? I should cut him out of my life. I never would have let any man treat me that way. But I did love him, after all. Perhaps he behaved this way because of his late wife, Sonya, because they had spent over a year in hospitals together.

I was at the hospital for three weeks. Mike called every day and couldn't understand why I had been hospitalized for such a long time. He kept saying: "Shosh, I love you very much. When are you coming to New York? I want you strong and healthy."

The last sentence annoyed me. What was he expecting? That I'd run a marathon? Go skydiving? I wasn't getting any younger, and neither was he. I thought that he wasn't aware of his old age.

My daughter, Galit, came to visit and brought coffee and croissants. They treated my pneumonia with antibiotics through an IV. My toe infection, on the other hand, was getting worse. The toe looked like an open and scarred wound. The toenail fell off, and they feared the skin around it might not regrow. I had a series of tests to make sure the bone wasn't damaged, and they wouldn't need to amputate. I had terrible edema around my knees and shins. My leg secreted liquid and the skin was very thin.

After three weeks of hospitalization, I went back home to my apartment on the third floor, up to which I had to climb 64 stairs. I was comforted by the fact that I would soon fly to New York, where things would be easier. But most importantly, I would be with Mike. On the other hand, I wasn't too eager to visit New York in the winter, it was very cold.

Mike told me that in late January three visitors from his Kiev clinic would visit him to attend a cardiology seminar. They would stay at his place until February 12. He suggested that I rest at home in the meantime and arrive on February 17.

My grandchildren were in daycare at the time. My grandson was in preschool and my granddaughter was still a toddler. Some of the moms were good friends with my daughter and started visiting us pretty often. They would visit on Fridays and even in the middle of the week. Almost all of them knew of my story with Mike, as Galit would talk openly about it. One of the mothers was Ukrainian, and very outgoing. When she heard the story about Mike's visitors from Kiev, she burst out laughing, and said (possibly spitefully): "He's probably fooling around with one of them, and the other two are her best friends."

I dismissed what she said. "Mike is a serious and respectable man, a learned man. That isn't his style."

However, her words seeped through my thoughts.

Another mom from my grandson's daycare, Smadar, started visiting us. She was a whole other story. She had non-identical twins, a boy and a girl. She was a pretty woman, friendly, and very lively, she was also chubby and had served in the army. In the past, she had been addicted to drugs and was homeless. The person who helped her get off the streets was a Palestinian man from a village next to Ramallah. He didn't have any permits and the police was after him. He saved her from her addiction.

He wanted to marry her, so she became a Muslim and got married according to Islamic law. A year after they married, she had the twins. Sometimes, she would drive to see her mother-in-law in the village in the occupied territories. His relatives would wait for her and protect her. Her mother was from the north. She is a sick woman who walked around with a small oxygen tank. Her father was a Greek businessman who had diabetes and was a bilateral amputee. He left his wife and ran off with his

Filipina caregiver. Every now and then he would send his wife and daughter some money. Smadar didn't work. She took care of the twins and received welfare. Her husband worked at the market in different temporary jobs. They stayed in a one-room apartment next to the market. When she would come to visit, her husband would call every ten minutes to ask when she would be home with the twins.

For my grandson's birthday, Smadar bought an impressive gift with the money she had received from her father. She too, thought it appropriate to remark about Mike and the Ukrainians. In the meantime, I heard she'd started walking with a hijab, as Muslim women often do.

That was my Galit, constantly seeing justice for everyone.

Every day, right on time, at my 3 PM and his 8 AM, Mike would Skype me from his home office in his basement. The women from Kiev cooked his breakfast in the kitchen, and they would call him once it was ready. He sent me some pictures of them. Two were in their sixties, not too attractive and rather clumsy. The third looked younger; she wasn't beautiful but somewhat attractive. She had brown hair and bright eyes. All I knew was that her name was Lara.

He told me about his daily schedule and said that the

night before he had taken them out to a Japanese restaurant. It was one of those places where the cooks slice and fry the food in a spectacular show in front of the diners. The girls were thrilled and shouted with excitement. I told him I would love to go there, too. I was impressed by how he handled business and pleasure at the same time. He ran to bring a box with Mandarin or Korean writing on it. He said that he was revealing his deepest secret: every morning he would drink ginseng elixir. "It energizes me," he said. The pack had fifty small glass cups with straws. I remembered that he brought one of those boxes with him when he came to visit and left it here for me. I drank the ginseng essence on a daily basis; at the hospital they couldn't figure out why my blood pressure spiked to 220. Then I realized it was because of the elixir and decided to stop. After a couple of days, my blood pressure stabilized. I decided to return the box once I visit him in New York.

I was starting to get ready for my visit. I had a visa for the States. I booked a flight for February 17. My travel agent recommended that I ask for a wheelchair on my flight to New York and on my way back. He said it would make the security checks and long halls much easier. It really did help. I was unaware that this service existed. I was asked to provide an estimated return date. However,

I didn't know whether I was visiting for two months or a longer period of time. The travel agent said I could always change the date, though it might cost me extra. I decided to travel premium class, which was between business and economy. I was asked to add eight hundred dollars for each direction, just so I could have some extra leg room and better meals. In hindsight, it was an unnecessary expense for very little comfort.

I started organizing the documents I was planning to take with me: two books I had begun to write, one of which was an updated version of a children's book, music sheets, and some music I had composed. Those were documents I had kept for years and were evidence of an entire lifetime. It was pretty difficult handling forty-year-old documents that I wanted to show Mike, some were old photos. I wanted to travel light, with the bare minimum.

I still hadn't completely recovered. I wasn't sure my toe would get back to what it used to be. I couldn't be sure that the skin surrounding it would grow back. My doctor recommended that due to my medical condition, I should take blood thinners for the flight, as I had recently battled a severe pneumonia. I told Mike that perhaps it was best if I postponed the visit and come at a later time, since I wasn't entirely healthy. He said that

I should come, and he would take care of me over there. If there would be any problem, he would take me to the hospital he was affiliated with. My legs still secreted liquids. The hems of my pants would occasionally become damp. That was also why I struggled wearing socks on my own. I hesitated. Mike would have to help me wear my socks.

Mike said that a couple of days after I'd arrive, we'd go to City Hall and get married. I panicked again. I wanted to live with him first, see how we lived by each other's side, and then decide how we would move forward. He was eager to get married. I couldn't understand why.

My relationship with my daughter was rather formal. I knew she was angry that I was leaving. The way she saw it, I was abandoning her and the grandchildren. I thought that as a woman, even an old one, I had the right live my life and love. I was more than just a sweet old grandma. She said that she and the kids would come to the airport with me.

On February 12, the Kiev visitors left. Mike told me about them every day. He said they were hard working women, studious and devoted to their work in his Kiev clinic, especially Lara, who ran the clinic. According to him, Lara was something special. Her uncle had participated in the Babi Yar Jewish massacre, while her father, had driven Jews to the killing pits. Since her childhood, Lara was remorseful for her relatives' cooperation with the Nazis and she wanted to atone for her family's crimes. Though she was a devout Christian and prayed to Jesus and the Virgin Mary, she was interested in Judaism and the Jewish people. She had gotten closer to the Jewish community, and even had many Jewish friends. She pleasantly assisted anyone she could and had done so for many years. I noticed that Mike's eyes sparkled whenever he would mention her name.

On the day of my flight to New York, I carefully wore my makeup and coiffed my hair. I looked good. I ordered a taxi and asked the driver to take down my suitcase and place it in the car. It was 6 AM. My daughter and grandchildren were sound asleep. I didn't want to wake them, so I kissed them and took my walker that was tied to the stairs at the entrance to the building. We drove to the airport.

I looked at the sights before me as if for the last time. I had a feeling this was goodbye. We arrived. I went through security at the entrance to the airport. The driver approached my airline's desk, and once he returned, he said that someone would come with a wheelchair and push me to all the way to airplane. And so it was. What a wonderful arrangement I hadn't known about. I could have flown to so many places around the world. I skipped the duty-free shops and remembered I could shop tax free on the plane.

The premium class seat was very comfortable, and the flight went by smoothly. People scared me about flying at my age for nothing. The food was tasty, but I don't think any of it justified the price difference. I didn't panic. I napped every now and then. I bought some Chivas whiskey and Hermes perfume.

I arrived pretty calm at JFK. I had a wheelchair again, so that all the security checks went by easily and quickly. I was one of the first people off the airplane. I sat and waited among all the greeters. I looked at the relatives who, one after the other, approached their loved ones or friends. After half an hour I noticed Mike who stood there with a luggage cart, slightly hunched over, wearing a black beret and a slightly wilted bouquet of dahlias. I walked to him and touched his shoulder, just as I had done on our first meeting at the Ben Gurion Airport. He turned around with a puzzled look. How could I have arrived so quickly? We hugged in length. He kissed me. We walked to the car that was parked close by.

A Village in the Heart of New York

We drove for half an hour and held hands at each stop. We drove by a cemetery. Then, we arrived at a suburban neighborhood comprised of narrow streets with lonely gray houses. We stopped in front of one of them, which was his house. There were three stairs between the front door and the house. We didn't even place our luggage in the living room before he swept me off my feet and hugged me. We kissed and then climbed up to the bedroom.

It was a master bedroom, with a comfy king-sized bed; just the way I like it. We snuggled under the sheets, as if nothing else mattered. I was his and he was mine. We were both overwhelmed with passion and yearning for one another. It was unconditional love. Time stood still as we lay embraced in each other's arms.

The house was rather disappointing. It was a gray and

without a front garden. In the backyard there were some poor flowers that resembled daffodils. The living room was packed with uncomfortable furniture: wide and low Texan-style sofas that you couldn't get up from, three-seats, two and one; two sideboards loaded with crystals and documents; small coffee tables with medical journals that had published his articles. There were photographs of his late wife Sonya and their children hanging on the walls. Plastic bags stuffed with different papers were lying around the house. The stairs leading up to the bedrooms were awkward and another flight of narrow stairs led down to his office basement. I was slightly angry at myself for criticizing him. He did his best to be a good host. The dining table was covered in groceries he had bought at the neighborhood Jewish supermarket, fresh fruits, bread, pastries and stuffed vegetables. I felt that I was needlessly whining, even about the toilet seats, that I thought were too narrow– not only in his house, but also in the restaurants we had visited. They were so shallow that occasionally, I could touch the water inside. I wasn't expecting that in America.

I had to stop being so critical. He tried so hard to please me, while I kept looking for problems. I should be happy. Be pleased that I was in the arms of the man I loved, enjoy the warmth of his body, his smooth skin;

all the rest was meaningless. I would love him even if we were in a shabby shack.

An Airlift

For some reason, I was rather suspicious of him. Something didn't sit right. But I couldn't put my finger on it. In the evening, we went to a big and quite lame supermarket. Mike thought I might need to get a couple things. It was very cold. The passages between the different isles were outdoors, so we kept going in and out from the cold wind. There wasn't anything special I wanted to buy. We just strolled around, and I kept wanting to sit down. There weren't any chairs or benches. This was the first time I noticed Mike starting to get aggravated.

When we returned home, I told Mike I was going upstairs, to the bedroom. Mike said he was going down to the basement and that he would come in a little while.

At night, in bed, we worked everything out. We hugged. I melted in his arms. We had wonderful sex. But I gradually realized this wasn't enough. This wasn't what life was about. I had to find a place in his life. I had to stop acting like a tourist and be his partner, his wife. I couldn't quite understand why a man of his stature, a famous and successful doctor, chose to live in such a remote and gray neighborhood instead of a large fancy house, adorned with works of art. He chuckled as he replied that a great part of his work is volunteer. He was funding the maintenance of both of his clinics. As such, he didn't want to live in a luxurious home. He had private parking, and everything he needed – he was content with his lot. All in all, he liked helping people less fortunate and find solutions for different medical conditions.

In the morning he woke up first, by force of habit, and made scrambled eggs with sliced vegetables – bell peppers, tomatoes, and onions. He bought delicacies in abundance, smoked salmon, fruits and fresh breads. I knew that I would need some time before I started to feel comfortable.

After breakfast he was off to take care of the clinic and I stayed home alone. I walked around. There were two guest bedrooms in addition to the master bedroom. There were many large portraits of Mike and Sonya hanging on the walls. The images from their youth were filled with affection and love. They held hands and supported each other. In later pictures, before Sonya became ill, she looked like an angel with a frozen smile. In one of her pictures with Mike, his arm is wrapped around her shoulder while hers are hanging by her body, not touching him.

I started unpacking my bags and suitcase and looked for a free drawer to place them in. I opened the drawers of the nightstand by my side of the bed. I found two crumpled towels with different stains that had dried. I threw them into a plastic laundry bag. There was a TV in every room, but none worked. I couldn't find a current newspaper around the house, so I couldn't tell what was going on. The computer Mike had installed for me wasn't working and we were waiting for the technician. In fact, aside from my phone, I was completely disconnected from the outside world. My Israeli phone wasn't working because Mike had promised to provide me with a local one. My daughter tried calling him and he told her that I had arrived, and everything was well.

And then, my mind wandered back to those towels and the Ukrainian women who had visited him. He only had two guest rooms, where did the third woman sleep? That was the only thing that bothered me in that moment. I assumed that the third one was Lara, who was better looking than the other two. My spying senses had already built an entire story. Was I exaggerating?

Have I nothing better to do than suspect that my Mike, my husband to be, had arranged an airlift of women for himself? The Ukrainian left on February 12, and me, the Israeli, landed in New York on February 17. Nothing short of an airlift.

I was even ashamed to be introduced to his relatives whom I was supposed to meet in a couple of days. My Mike, a second-rate Don Juan.

Perhaps I was just imagining things and Mike, an eighty-five-year-old man who was very well-groomed, indeed wanted to build a new life with me.

We could quickly see the differences between us. He ran up and down the stairs like a child, while I could barely climb each single stair. My health condition wasn't stable. I should have postponed my visit and not come in the winter. My legs were swollen, and the hems of my pants would become damp because of the liquids. I had to frequently change the bandages on my injured toe.

So many thoughts crossed my mind. Assuming he was sleeping around with Lara and was having an affair with her for several years, then, it would seem that she slept in his bedroom. He spent each night in her arms. Then, every morning at 8 AM he would go down to the basement to talk and flirt with me until the Ukrainians called him for breakfast. I thought it wasn't fair to me or Lara.

He wanted to buy me a piano since he knew I liked to play. I couldn't see any place where we could place a piano. I decided to wash the breakfast dishes. Perhaps I'd cook a rich stew or something. He had a sophisticated fridge with two doors and completely packed. I couldn't find any fresh vegetables in it. Both fresh and rotten vegetables were stored together. I'd already noticed it, as a child who had suffered from hunger during the Holocaust, he hated throwing food out. He just couldn't. All the kitchen drawers were filled with expired powders and spices. There were dozens of old pill bottles on the shelves in the corner. I noticed little bugs walking freely in some places in the kitchen. I gave up on making the stew. Perhaps I'd make some pasta. Luckily, I found a drawer stuffed with canned goods. I found an Italian tomato sauce and on a different shelf, I found some recently bought pasta. He had a large number of good-quality pots. I was about to boil the water for the pasta and wanted to open the Italian tomato sauce when I noticed the expiration date: it was for 2005. One moment… its 2019 now. I gave up on making pasta.

There were many plastic bags lying around the kitchen floor. At first, I couldn't quite understand why. I decided to collect all the bags and throw them into one of the bins. Everything was clean around. I was pleased with what I had done.

In the evening, Mike came back with groceries. He unpacked what he had bought and placed some of the items in the fridge. I noticed that he left the empty bags on the kitchen floor.

I remember that Alex, my husband, had the same experiences in his childhood, but I didn't sense from him what I did from Igor. Alex loved meat; I would buy large quantities of meat and bones to cook him a meat broth with beats and roots. Most of the time, Alex was happy and kind, he always wanted to appear successful as a businessman and loved walking around with large rolls of money.

After he'd closed a big deal, he would place the money on the table in front of me. "Here, take it," he would say and take a couple of notes for gas and cigarettes.

Both Alex and Igor were some of the last twenty-year-old Holocaust survivors; soon enough there wouldn't be any Holocaust survivors left. A whole world disappearing into the mists of time.

A Dash of Evil and Wandering Mice

In the morning, after breakfast, we drove to Manhattan. We arrived to Fifth Avenue, in front of the Plaza Hotel and Central Park. We drove by the Trump Building. Mike suggested we continue by foot. We couldn't find parking. I suggested that I'd walk around by myself and we'd meet again at an excellent Jewish deli on 47th Street, and then we'd go on a cruise facing the Manhattan skyline reflected off the water.

In the evening, Mike decided he'd take me to Chinatown in Queens. All the signs and streets were in Chinese. We found an authentic Chinese restaurant, there were Chinese and Korean diners. I didn't like the food. I preferred Giraffe," the Asian restaurant in Tel Aviv. At the end of the meal, a waitress placed a takeaway bag in my hand, without me asking for it, with a green jelly string salad we didn't like. Mike parked far away and asked that I wait for him by the restaurant. It was very cold outside. I leaned against the restaurant fence. We were on an intersection and I finally noticed that there were dozens of rats scattering on the road and sidewalk; people kept on going as if it were nothing. I was tired and cold. I looked at my watch. I saw that it had been more than half an hour and Mike still hadn't arrived. He couldn't have parked that far. I put the takeaway bag with the alien-looking salad aside. I waited. I had a strange feeling, as if Mike was sitting quietly in the car close by, watching me stand and suffer in the cold, leaning helplessly against the sidewalk banister.

Another fifteen minutes passed. Suddenly, Mike's car appeared and stopped next to me. I stepped into the car with mixed feelings. I didn't say a thing. Actions spoke louder than words. Mike smiled at me. When we stopped in front of the traffic light, he squeezed my hand warmly. I wanted to have some coffee and a comforting cinnamon Danish; there were none of those around.

Mike asked what I'd like to do next day. I asked him to check which opera was playing at the Met and buy tickets. He promised that he would.

When we returned home, my leg began to hurt terribly. He examined it and said that I must have pulled something in my knee and that I should lie back with my feet up high. He said it would ease the pain. He also recommended that I take some painkillers. He made me some tea and I told him I would go upstairs to rest. He said he would go to work in the basement and check his emails.

I was happy to stay in the bedroom by myself and relax, snuggled under the blanket. I didn't want to think of a thing. I knew that Mike would come to bed late. I knew that he was going to work, but at midnight, rather than coming to bed, he goes to the kitchen, washes the dishes and rests for two hours on the recliner in the living room.

I asked him once, "Are you avoiding me?"

He laughed and caressed my head. "Silly, I'm resting in the living room because I need my hours of sleep, otherwise, I wouldn't be able to function the next day."

"You can sleep in the bedroom, why sleep in the living room?"

"I can't sleep when I'm next to you. You arouse me…" he said.

"We don't have to make love every night," I said.

"But the problem is that I want you so much, and so do you," Mike said.

For some reason, I didn't buy it.

A Prenup

Mike came to breakfast armed with a dossier of documents. "Shosh, I want to show you something. It's a prenup, and I'd like you to sign it before we go to City Hall. Let me explain; from the day you landed here in New York, you'll receive three thousand dollars a month, for life. If something were to happen to me, and I die before you, you'll receive two thousand dollars every month, which is the sum of my American social security. My kids and their families will receive the assets, houses, and the apartments in Miami and California."

I replied that I agreed and was willing to sign.

We finished eating our breakfast and Mike left for his clinic.

I kept sipping from my coffee, not wanting to think of a thing. Why did I agree to sign that? There was only one reason for this: I came here to be with him for a trial period, and there were some things that weren't to my liking. Regardless if I signed or not. The offer didn't make sense, but I didn't want to argue. If he passes away before I do, two thousand dollars wouldn't suffice for my living costs. Plus, I'd lose all my rights in Israel, though I was quite sure I'd pass away before he does. I decided, that despite loving him very deeply, I wasn't ready to get married at the moment. I wanted to be with him and spend time with him. I wanted him as a lover, but not as a husband. Furthermore, I wasn't willing to be the good and devoted wife who spent her life standing politely in different ceremonies, listening to speeches by different acclaimed people as I implore for a chair to sit on. I thought that I had to wait when it came to crucial decisions. People don't always get married at our age. I wanted to enjoy my stay in New York, as much as my medical condition would allow it. I also wanted to go to the apartment in Miami, escape from the Big Apple's harsh winter. I feared that we'd ruined all the wonderful things we were building together.

Mike returned after a couple of hours; he was all smiles. He walked into the house, waving around pieces of paper. "I got tickets for *Aida* at the Met. We're going tonight. We should leave early for Manhattan, so we make it on time."

From the Highest of Heights
to the Lowest of Lows

We left for Manhattan at around 5 PM. We arrived at the Met, and I could recognize from a distance the fountain that was featured in *Moonstruck* starring Cher. It was very cold outside. My foot hurt and I struggled to walk. Mike went to park the car. He gave me my ticket and said we'd meet inside.

I asked one of the ushers to help me reach my seat, because I was struggling to walk. He said he'd immediately send someone to help me up the elevator. I waited for a couple of minutes, and then came a chubby usher wearing a bowtie. I handed him my ticket, so he'd take me to my seat. He looked at it and slightly sulked. I could tell that this wasn't a fancy seat. We passed across hallways with red carpets. On the second floor, I saw people sitting around round tables covered in perfect tablecloths with crystal vases, waiting for their dinner to be served. It's a shame that Mike hadn't thought about it. I would have enjoyed eating there.

I walked out of the elevator and to the stairs leading to my seat. I climbed up the stairs and showed the ticket to the usher that handed out programs. He pointed at my seat that was one row before the last. I had to climb up dozens of stairs with my aching leg. I looked around me and was mortified. I hoped that I wouldn't be seen by any acquaintances.

The seats, known as Family Circle seating, were close to the ceiling, right in front of the famous chandeliers that would be lifted up once the concert begins. I saw Mike sitting up and smiling at me.

I almost wanted to run away. I started climbing up the stairs, my foot hurt terribly, I groaned with every step. I had never sat in such terrible seats at the opera, not in Paris or in Milan. Those couldn't have been the last tickets he found. There must have been better seats. It would have been better if we hadn't gone at all.

Nonetheless, there was a good view from anywhere in the Met. The production was impressive. For the finale, there were real horses and carriages on stage. Earlier, during the intermission, rather than sitting next to me, Mike climbed up to the last row, claiming there was more light for him there to look through the program. That was the last straw.

Mike returned to his seat before the intermission was over. 'What was he really doing up there?' I asked myself. 'Was he reading the program, or did he make a phone call?' I berated myself instead of having a good time. I was in the Met in Manhattan, watching *Aida*. I sat there feeling extremely frustrated, staring at the famous chandeliers that had been lifted up to the sound of the crowd's ovations.

Afterward, I went down with Mike to the parking. He asked me sit on a bench at the entrance and said he would bring the car as he had parked very far, and I would struggle walking there. I sat there, clutching my purse. That was where I kept my passport, money and phone. He started heading to the parking lot and then suddenly turned around. He took my bag and said that he had to drive around a couple of blocks, as he would have to leave the parking and drive back through a different street. There was a kind employee there who explained to him how he would leave the parking and return in a different way. People started arriving to the parking lot that was slowly emptying. I sat there without my bag, money, phone or hope. I couldn't understand why Mike would take my purse. Perhaps he was worried because someone might try to steal it from me. I don't know. All I knew was that I sat there alone and freezing for two hours. I started thinking what I would do if he didn't come back and simply abandoned me there. Me, a purse-less 82-year-old lady, no documents, no money, alone in the frozen Big Apple, sick and weak with a scarred toe. I was very concerned. Two hours? What was Mike doing out there for two whole hours? Was it so hard to find his way back? After all, he was a New Yorker.

'Perhaps he met someone or some women in the parking lot?' I thought. 'Anything is possible!'

I had made up my mind: I will not marry this man, no matter what.

I should have prepared my visit more thoroughly. I had to provide at least one address of an acquaintance in New York, a place I could escape to if something went wrong. And indeed, as far as I was concerned, something had gone wrong.

I sat alone in front of the parking employee, who also began to worry. Soon his shift was over. There weren't any cars left in the parking lot. What would I do if they closed? Where would I go? I didn't even have money for a cup of coffee. Perhaps I turn to the police? Or the Israeli Embassy? I had almost made up my mind.

Suddenly, Mike's car appeared in front of me. He

handed me the purse and said that he couldn't find the entrance to where I was sitting, which is why he had to drive around. I didn't reply. I didn't say a word. All I did was ask: "Why did you take my purse?"

He said that he was concerned that if I'd be alone with my purse, someone would try to steal it or hurt me.

I was both physically and mentally exhausted. I couldn't muster the strength to think and make up my mind. Should I spend some more time in New York and join him on a visit to tropical Miami? Or should I take off back to Israel? But I hadn't come all this way to New York only to leave three days later. I didn't have the powers for that, either. I was feeling drained from the pain in my leg, toe and the antibiotics. I couldn't fly now. Plus, the love I had for him was still there. I also felt he wasn't too excited about our trip to Miami. The way he had treated me was bordering on hatred – love and hate. Perhaps everything that happened at the parking lot was to show me that I wasn't wanted, and I should take the hint.

I left the parking lot and followed him to the car. I looked back at the bench where I had spent the last two hours. I felt that a part of me was still sitting there at the Met parking lot, as if I were one of the ghosts haunting New York City.

I sat in the car silently, my hands hanging by my sides. I didn't say a word. There was nothing to say aside from complaining, so I kept quiet. I didn't touch him. He also kept silent the entire way home. I climbed up to the bedroom to rest. He went to his basement office and stayed there for an hour. Then he came up to the bedroom. He embraced me in his arms and kissed me goodnight. I kissed him back.

I slept in the next morning. When I came downstairs, Mike had prepared me a rich breakfast. He had made my coffee just the way I liked it. The bread was properly toasted and smeared with whipped butter, very American. Slices of smoked salmon, lemon, a salad and omelet, were all served on fancy plates. Mike really went the extra mile. He said he'd come to pick me up for lunch. I told him I wanted to talk to him when he returned.

For lunch we went to a nice Italian restaurant. Mike had a habit of ordering one main course for the both of us, because the dishes were very generous in the States. He loved pasta with chunks of beef, while I preferred spinach. I let him have his way. I don't like pasta with meat. He put some on my plate and I barely touched it. I ordered a mango margarita. The waitress came back with a large round cup filled with extremely sweet mango margarita. I drank half of it. But I couldn't drink anymore. I had diabetes, so it was a good idea for me to stop.

Mike was annoyed, "You have to finish it. I hate it when we waste food."

"Look, Mike dear, I'd rather that the sugar left in the cup won't affect my blood system. It's pure sugar. I had some, I enjoyed it, and that's that. I don't want to have anymore, I have diabetes."

He mumbled some words to himself in response.

"Mike, my love, we're over eighty, but your eighties aren't the same as mine. We each have our own habits. We won't change and let us not try to change one another, otherwise we'll have to break this up and go our separate ways."

"Shosh, enough, I love you."

"So love me, '*enough*.' We don't have time for these games. You won't change me, and I won't change you. We need to talk."

"Right, you need to sign the documents, and then we'll go to City Hall. Okay, Shosh, my love?"

"Mike, we need to talk about everything before we go to Miami."

"As you wish, Shosh Kinneret, my dear."

Revealing Deep Secrets

It was after midnight. We embraced each other in the king size bed.

"Mike, I wanted to talk to you about Alex. Did you finally meet, like you had planned to?"

For some reason, Mike was embarrassed again.

"Yes, Shosh, we did."

"When?"

"We met at the Red Square in Moscow, in August 1977."

"Interesting, Mike, very interesting. I remember Alex going on a long trip. It was a special time. It was also the only time I suspected that Alex cheated on me."

Mike looked down. He was embarrassed. Something about his look and body language revealed something that neither him nor Alex dared tell me.

"Why do you think that Alex cheated on you, and why

then, of all times?"

"Very simple, I was on pregnancy bedrest, and we hadn't had sex in a few months. And Alex, as you well know, isn't made out of sugar."

"Shosh, that's no reason to suspect him. Did you speak to him about this?"

"No, never."

"Then why do you want to cause yourself bitter disappointment? Perhaps there was nothing and it's all in your head?"

"Mike, there was something going on, and I'm sure of it. And according to your and Alex's body language, I'm guessing that there's some truth to it, and that you know something. It embarrasses me. Tell me what you think you know."

"Shosh, I know nothing." Mike looked down again.

I wanted to know. At any cost.

"Shosh, my love, let us remember Alex favorably. You loved each other. Why is it so important for you to know?"

"I want to know. I have to hear. I felt that Alex regretted something that had happened."

"Shosh, it's hard for me to talk about it. But if you insist – it's at your own risk.

"Like I said, Shosh, we met in Moscow. It was a very

moving and empowering meeting. Alex had some time to stay with me. I was supposed to leave for the clinic in Kiev, but I received a call about a sick child in Monrovia and I told Alex that I had to go to Africa. Alex asked if he could join me because we didn't know when we'd meet again. We traveled to Kiev. I added to our journey two nurses from the clinic and we headed there. In Africa, I took care of the sick boy. He had a complicated surgery in Monrovia, and everything ended peacefully. We stayed, however, to monitor his condition. After work, we walked around for a while. We visited some gold and diamond mines, nature reserves and some good restaurants in Monrovia, where mostly diamond traders dined. There were also some Israeli traders and licensed commercial loggers. That's it, Shosh."

"What, that's it? Where's the catch? What exactly happened?"

"You're stubborn Shosh, and you're going to regret it."

"Mike, I won't let go until you tell me. What were the names of the kind Kiev nurses who joined you to Africa?"

"Anastasia and Lara; happy?"

For some reason, I was reminded of the crumpled-up towels I found in Mike's nightstand. 'What a coincidence,' I thought.

Mike's story distracted me from my stressful Met incident.

"Okay, back to our story? Or 'back to our sheep' as they say in French." I said.

"At your own risk, Shosh. I don't know if I'm even allowed to tell you all this," Mike said.

"At night, we would occasionally walk on the beach. There was a pleasant ocean breeze. The wet season hadn't begun yet, the rainy season. The beach was right next to the hotel, where we stayed in comfortable bungalows. One night, I wanted to chat with Alex and headed to his bungalow. The door was open. The curtains blew in the wind and Alex stood in the room, naked, next to the wide bed that was covered in a white mosquito net. Alex was so handsome, he looked like a Greek God under the moonlight. I wanted to walk in and talk to him, when I suddenly saw Lara – her red hair spread on the pillow, her breasts jiggled as your Alex was bending over her. I took a step back. I was shocked. I don't think that Alex noticed me. I left."

"So, you've both slept with Lara?!"

"Enough, Shosh! That's it!"

"I should send her friend request on Facebook, so we can share experiences."

Mike laughed.

"You share your women," I said. "You even told me once that your wife, Sonya, used to know Alex and was in love with him."

"That's not true. I said that Alex was so kind and good-looking that if my wife, Sonya, would have met him, she would have fallen for him."

My Alex, my beloved husband.

Contemplating on the Way to Miami

In a couple of days, we leave for Miami. The plan was to go on the I-95 and drive all the way to Florida. We expected the trip to be three days. If we had time, we'd visit a couple of his friends. When we arrive in Florida, we can go visit Cape Canaveral, and perhaps we'd even see the March launch of the Beresheet spaceship.

As long as we didn't talk about getting married at City Hall, the stress between us faded, but uncertainty was still there.

He lived at a remote area and it was impossible to commute without a car. The island of Manhattan was where I wanted to be. I had a feeling that I was living in a distant village. The way I saw it; he wasn't living in New York.

Plus, I couldn't figure out our relationship. I knew that he loved me and that I was crazy for him. He didn't want to lose me either. At his age, despite all the widowers and divorcees fawning over him, he wasn't sure he'd meet his soulmate. We shouldn't miss each other, but the price was too high.

I had a difficult dilemma. I love him very much. He drove me insane. There was a side to him that I couldn't understand, one that including a hint of evil, despite all his kindness and generosity. Okay, so even though he kept making "threats" that he'd retire, he kept working. But what was the deal with him disappearing every night for a long time? He worked in the basement, came up to do the dishes and then nap on the living room sofa. Anything but come upstairs! I didn't know whether I could live with that. Was that a control thing? There was more to it. I come to you whenever I want to make love to you and you're always ready and willing. I could have made love to him every day. I've never rejected him, complained of a headache or anything of the like. I loved him, was crazy about being close to him. I couldn't explain what was happening. I waited for him in bed like a dummy, waiting for him to come back from the basement. If he loved me, how could he behave like that?

This has nothing to do with my daughter, but sometimes, the things he did were bordering on sadism and emotional abuse. It was Galit who had seen through it, which was why she was hostile toward him. She couldn't understand what was happening to me and why I had given in so willingly.

He claimed that he was staying in the basement and living room for long hours because he needed his sleep. I didn't know whether I should buy into it. If you ask me, if he thought he could treat me that way, he didn't know me one bit. Didn't he know I was better than that?

I wasn't willing that any man would treat me this way. As I had said, I loved him, was attracted to him, loved hearing his voice and spending time with him. He would also help me put on my socks and shoes; something I had imposed on him by coming here sick. And yet, I could see slight elements of abuse. Did it have to do with his Holocaust childhood? Alex had survived the Holocaust too, and yet, I'd never felt a smidgen of evil in him. He was the epitome of kindness.

In fact, his abuse started the first day I arrived. He didn't take me on trips or tours like he did the Ukrainians. He simply took off the very next day and left me alone for five hours with no TV or computer. He just left me here, as if saying 'screw off'.

It felt like he was disrespecting me. He took me for granted! That was definitely disrespectful, especially toward the woman you want to build a life with and marry, the woman who had come to you in her old age, over eighty, after having suffered severe pneumonia and an injury, in terrible cold weather. She came to be with you and see whether she could have a life with you. And all this happened on the very first day. What were his priorities?

What would come next?

What would happen tomorrow?

Miami

We took the I-95 to Florida. It took us more than three days to get to Miami, because we stopped in Washington. We drove through North and South Carolina. We stayed in motels and different inns. Mike made sure we always had a comfortable king size bed and a rich breakfast, usually a buffet. We stopped talking about the wedding for the meantime, and we both felt lighter. We ate in nice diners and well-known chain restaurants. Mike would always order one main course and we'd share it. As mentioned, I didn't like it.

One time, on Long Island, he ordered a seafood meal containing salmon, other seafood and some lobster. Mike, who didn't like the seafood, just took the salmon for himself. Frankly, I wanted to have some, but he gave me the rest of the seafood and lobster.

The weather kept changing all the way to Florida.

I took off my warm coat and wore a jean jacket and summer clothes.

We finally reached Miami. Mike's apartment was located in an impressive 500-apartment building. It was a one-bedroom apartment, splendid and well-kept, it also had a dining room and a living room with a mirror-covered wall and a widescreen TV. An exquisite bottle of red wine waited for us on the table; a gift from his granddaughter and her husband who had stayed there a couple of weeks before.

Sadly, I thought the bedroom was rather disappointing. Instead of a simple king size bed, there was an elegant bed trapped in a walnut wood frame. It was covered in a shimmery black satin cover, with a print of a tall bird, probably a stork. The glimmering black satin reminded me of a funeral home.

It was hard lying under the cover, that Mike insisted we leave on the bed, let alone have an orgasm. I thought the cover was nothing more than an obstacle. The cover radiated negative energy. There was an empty water bottle with a picture of a rose on it next to the bed.

I was still aroused. Mike took a shower. I removed the shiny black fabric. I took advantage of that fact that Mike wasn't there, and I snatched the empty bottle. The mouth of the bottle fit perfectly into my vagina, which was completely wet. I came very shortly.

After having suffered from the cold weather in the Big Apple, Miami agreed with me. We walked by the ocean and visited Fort Lauderdale, which I liked very much. We had dinner at a Polynesian restaurant and watched a fascinating Hawaiian dance performance. The performance was mesmerizing and thought provoking. There were many pina coladas served to our table, but I was the only one doing the drinking, because Mike was driving. We shared a fish dish with rice, tropical fruits and a secret sweet and sour sauce, and yet another delicacy. It was raining outside. I was slightly tipsy when we came back. This time, I climaxed quickly, despite the black glossy cover.

After breakfast, Mike worked by the dining table, facing the mirrored wall. I watched TV. I was surprised to find "The Young and the Restless" episodes; the show hadn't been broadcast in Israel in fourteen years. I was happy to see it. It was like having a reunion with old friends. Victor was still alive and kicking, though filled with Botox, and Nicky was still involved in different scandals. In the afternoon we went down to the pool, and then to the marina. Later, we drove to a large restaurant and food court and ate at a Russian restaurant, which I rather liked. This time, we each ordered our own main course, I ordered the Beef Stroganoff and Mike had a salt-baked fish. Then we went to a hairdresser and I had my highlights done. Mike waited patiently. He read through scientific journals he had brought with him and went over his research and other articles.

On the days Mike was busy, I spent my time with *The Flame*, a Leonard Cohen poetry book that included some of his amazing songs and illustrations. His words spoke to everything I had gone through, as if Leonard Cohen were in my mind. I didn't have to go too far in my thoughts. Leonard did it for me. I concluded that love, with all its merits and disadvantages, does indeed, overcomes all.

Our stay in Miami was about to end. Luckily, I found a luxury store in the center of Miami and bought the perfume I had been using for years, Shalimar by Guerlain. Now I could start preparing my return home. I didn't purchase anything big. I looked for some cashmere sweaters to refill my stock. Each sweater was about one hundred dollars. I spent almost five hundred dollars on nothing but cashmere sweaters. Mike took me to simpler stores too and asked if I needed anything. I replied that I didn't need a thing. Sometimes, cheap could cost you. Even on my visit to London, I went to Harrods and bought a couple of cashmere sweaters. That was all I bought there, clothing wise. I also purchased two Staffordshire Spaniel dog figurines at an antique fair.

It was time to think about the next step.

Things Got Complicated

We returned to Mike's house. He said he'd check in on his clinic, though he got a full report while we were in Miami. He asked that I sign all the documents and after breakfast we'd go to City Hall to get married.

That was it. The dye had been cast.

I put on a white suit. My eyes sparkled. I looked wonderful. I bouquet. In short – we were going to get married and live happily ever after.

This is where the story should have ended, with a happy ending like a Hollywood movie. Things didn't play out that way.

After breakfast, I told Mike that I'd decided to return to Israel, then, of all times, just when the weather in New York was getting better. Mike looked at me in wonder. I told him that we mustn't get married now, and that we'd regret it later. I wouldn't be one hundred percent happy, and neither would he. I told him that I love him very much. I wasn't even aware of how much, or why. And I might regret my decision later on.

Mike was naturally very stubborn. He told me that if I had decided that we wouldn't marry, then he didn't know how long he'd keep pulling in that direction. I told him that was a risk I was willing to take. He said he'd always love me, and perhaps we shouldn't completely break things off. He would still be my lover and we'd meet every now and then in Tel Aviv or New York. He emphasized that his house would always be open to me.

I thought that these were things that people said to each other when they broke up. I was both relieved and agonized. I started missing him even before we parted ways. He hugged me and said that we weren't breaking things off but rather postponing our decision. I decided to return home April 3, 2019.

On the night before my flight, Mike took me to the Korean area of Chinatown in Queens. The signs were in Chinese. I couldn't tell between Chinese and Korean anyway. We drove down a main street. Mike wanted me to choose a restaurant according to its appearance. I couldn't understand his behavior. I would have rather stayed at home. Why wasn't he taking me to some place he knew?

We finally left the Korean area. Mike stopped by a Greek diner. The owner, a stout middle-aged man, was rather unpleasant and had what I thought to be somewhat of an anti-Semitic smile. I wanted to get up and leave, but Mike insisted that we stay. He ordered fish stuffed with shrimps and cream. I tasted it. It was disgusting. Mike ate the fish and was puzzled as to why I didn't touch the shrimps. I left everything in my plate. He was annoyed and ordered some orange juice for me, but I barely drank any. That was it, I was *"passé composé"* to him. We had coffee for dessert. He gestured with his hand, telling me to get up, it was time to go. He was trying to demonstrate domination, state that he was the decision-maker.

'Never mind, it doesn't matter' I thought to myself. I took a deep breath.

We went back home. I made sure that the bag, the suitcase and the presents for my grandchildren were packed and ready for the following day. We didn't speak. I went to sleep, and Mike went to work in the basement. This time, I fell asleep before he came up to bed in the middle of the night. He woke me up and began caressing me. I knew this was the last time we'd make love. I didn't know how long it would be before we saw each other again, if ever.

I don't want to get into any details.

It was wonderful. It was dramatic. We both cried!

***

The next day we ate breakfast quietly. Mike took the luggage to the car. At 10 AM we drove to JFK. Mike approached the El Al desk and I sat in the car. He came back with a crewmember and a wheelchair that people my age could have. The crewmember took the suitcase and bags. Mike and I hugged and lightly kissed goodbye. Suddenly, I had an inexplicable feeling, as if it were a "good riddance" kind of goodbye to Mike. He could have stayed with me by the El Al desk and walked me to the gate, but he chose to leave as quickly as possible and disappear into the Big Apple.

I the crewmember wheeled me to the El Al desk. One of the attendants weighed the suitcase, the three bags and the gift box. She said that my baggage was overweight and that I had to pay a fee of three hundred dollars. She explained that if I'd had a bigger suitcase, I could have saved the additional fee.

I was shocked. Why didn't Mike let me know that I had too many bags? I did eventually pay the extra fee. I didn't want to give up on the presents for my grandchildren, or the important paperwork I had in one of the bags. Next time, if there indeed would be a next time, I'd know to come better prepared.

Mike made sure that I had a special taxi waiting for me in Israel, and that the driver would take the luggage up to my apartment. He gave me some Israeli money for that; four hundred shekels. I knew it was too much, but I kept quiet.

This time I flew economy. There were two vacant seats next to me, so I could sleep for a while. It was better than premium; I had a special facility to place my legs but didn't have a gourmet meal. The food was rather tasty as it was, despite the fact I didn't have an appetite.

A driver waited for me at the Ben Gurion airport. When we reached my building, he took the suitcases to the third floor.

Seeing Galit was wonderful. She was very pleased that I had finally come back home. The grandchildren were even happier to see me and were expecting the presents I had showed them a couple of days earlier when we Skyped from New York. It was a grand "homecoming." Mike called in the afternoon to make sure I had arrived safely and that everything was fine.

Mike Opened all My Chakras

I couldn't tell what life would be like without Mike. Even if we would see each other again soon, it would only be in a couple of months. A couple of days had passed, but I still didn't begin to miss him. We spoke on the phone, however not every day. I was too busy with my reunion with Galit and my bright and adorable grandchildren; it was a different kind of bliss. I enjoyed seeing my only daughter excel in her business and create gorgeous, original pieces of jewelry and art in her store.

'She is going to take the world by storm', I thought to myself.

I organized everything I had brought back with me in the closets. I went down every morning to the café, read newspapers and did my crosswords. I sat alone.

I didn't have any patience to chat with friends or gossip. Sometimes, Mike would call at noon when I was still sitting in the café.

We spoke, I was pleased. We stayed in touch, but something had broken between us, and I was aching.

It was already Passover. I spent time with my daughter, my grandchildren, and with Shulamit, my good friend from Rehovot who taught and researched at the Weizmann Institute, and with her spouse of recent years, Jonathan. He was also a scientist, a handsome, muscular and dark man in his seventies,. We once again went to a fish restaurant at the Tel Aviv port. When we ordered dessert, my grandchildren told the waiter that is was their birthday. It wasn't true at all, but the dessert came with glitter, a candle and a "Happy Birthday" soundtrack! The children were overjoyed.

My friend, Shulamit, told me she was about to have an unpleasant surgery, a hysterectomy, and that she would have to rest for several weeks afterward. She chose to do it now because she was on a sabbatical.

Shulamit knew of my story with Mike. Sometimes, I'd call her from New York, and we'd talk. She knew all the little anecdotes and my hesitation. She and her partner, Jonathan, thought that Mike didn't treat me well, and they thought he was nothing more than a schmuck. They would say it to my face, when I'd try to play things down and tell them Mike was a generous and amazing person who had helped me greatly, and that he was an important figure in the Jewish community in New York, he was noble, fair and honorable. I didn't want to start wallowing and missing him. When I was reminded of him, I would cry, and I didn't want my mascara to run, so I tried not to think about him. I had a feeling that the months I had spent with him, which included a regular and steady sex life, simply opened all my chakras. No matter what, I needed a man's touch in my life, a hug, a kiss and a fuck. Plain and simple.

I was never lacking in suitors, but I couldn't jump into bed with just anyone. I knew that something would happen someday soon. I didn't know how, why or who with.

I started being active on Facebook, though at first, I couldn't quite understand the point of it. I added new friends. I made sure to add people of quality, both men and women. I would choose intellectuals, writers, artists and media people. We would discuss current events, and I was also rather active regarding the recurring elections. I was also in touch with a friend from Egypt, a Muslim man who spoke Hebrew and studied at the Cairo University. He would send me greetings daily. I explained to him I was an old woman, and he said that he was happy to greet me, keep in touch and correspond in Hebrew.

One day, I noticed Jonathan started sending me cards, hearts and flowers. It seemed rather strange. I didn't reciprocate in the same manner; I was simply surprised.

He was the spouse of my best friend of many years. What was going on? After all, I wouldn't have an affair with my best friend's partner. It wasn't ethical. Finally, he called me through WhatsApp.

"Shosh, why won't you answer me?"

"I don't understand," I replied. "What is the meaning of all this?"

"It means that Mike treated you poorly and Shulamit is right, so I wanted to put a smile on your face. Frankly, I've always admired you."

"Okay, thank you," I replied.

Jonathan kept greeting me good morning every day and would send images of coffee and flowers. I couldn't tell where this was going. I didn't reply. I felt bad for Shulamit, my good friend, who I adored. I could never hurt her.

Jonathan

My phone rang. I didn't pick up. A couple minutes later, the home phone rang. This time I did pick up. It couldn't have been Mike; it was nighttime on the East Coast.

Jonathan was on the line. "Shosh, why won't you pick up? Why won't you talk to me?"

"Jonathan, what do you want?"

"You!"

"Jonathan, as far as I'm concerned, you're my best friend's husband. What are you thinking? What could possibly happen between us? Yes, I was hurt in New York. But I was also to blame for what had happened. I love Mike, despite it all."

"Shosh, don't you realize he has abandoned you? That he treated you wrongly? Why won't you see the truth? If he truly loved you, he wouldn't have treated you that way. He wouldn't have let you come back to Israel."

"But Jonathan, I was the one who broke it off, I was the one who didn't want to get married now. I am to blame! Let's not dwell on spilled milk, I still don't know a thing. Perhaps I'll go to New York again in the summer," I replied. "I'm mad at you too. Why are you calling me in such a manner? What about Shulamit?"

"Shosh, do you want to hear the truth? The whole truth?"

"Yes, certainly, Jonathan."

"So you better sit down. This whole thing was her idea!"

"Whose?"

"Shulamit's!"

"So why hasn't she spoken to me about it? I can't believe it."

"She doesn't want to talk about it, or hear about it. She just wants the project to take its course."

It was hard for me to believed that Shulamit would think of such an idea. She had always been rather reserved when it came to matters of the heart. It was actually hard to make her talk.

"You're joking!" I said. "That's not nice. This is an absurd story."

"Okay, Shosh, let me explain. You know that she's about to have a surgery, right? So, due to her medical condition, she won't be able to have sex for a couple of months.

She thought about you, and what you've been through lately. She didn't want me to abstain from women, nor did she want me to be with women we don't know. With you, her best friend, it's like levirate marriage from the Jewish law. You're like a sister to her."

It was hard for me to accept this story, but somehow, I was convinced. Or at least I hoped to be.

"I'm either going to New York in the summer, or Mike will come here."

"Why should you go to New York when there are people who want you here?"

"I'm not looking for a relationship or a fling."

"I'm not looking for a relationship, either. I have a wife, a spouse. But she's sick at the moment. What do you think your Mike is doing? Do you think he's sitting at home and not meeting anyone? He might be with someone this very moment."

"Perhaps," I replied.

"Shosh, what the hell do you think. That your Mike, that eighty-five-year-old man, would fly across the ocean to get laid?"

"I would!" I responded, "There is more to it than just getting laid. I love this man."

"You would have crossed oceans because you're a romantic woman. He wouldn't," Jonathan said.

"Jonathan, that's not what we have – we love each other. I love that old man."

"Shosh, there are people here who love you, and I'm one of them."

"Jonathan, this is ridiculous! I can't keep talking about this. Besides, do you know how old I am? I'm ten years your senior."

"Shosh, age is just a number. You look at least twenty years younger. Besides, I desire you."

"Jonathan, good night!"

An hour passed. Jonathan called again.

"Shosh, I'm coming over tomorrow at three. Make sure you have coffee and cake," Jonathan said and hung up.

I sat there, surprised by the turn our conversation had taken. I didn't respond. I heard an incoming text on my phone. The time was 3 AM. I sat down to have my coffee; I won't be sleeping tonight. I opened the phone and saw a text from Jonathan with a picture I had to download. I downloaded it and was shocked.

The man had sent me a closeup of his penis fully erect.

I felt as though I had just been slapped. I felt cheap. I felt like a slut.

'Rude,' I thought.

Crime and Punishment

I woke up with mixed feelings. Even after coffee, I'd managed to sleep for a couple of hours. I didn't think of a thing, not even about Mike. I had an omelet, salad, and a cup of coffee. I listened to the news, then folded Galit's and the grandchildren's laundry. I cleaned my room, changed my sheets and pillow covers. Then I ordered groceries for delivery. I replaced the soap in the bathroom sink. Once someone told me about the many things that can be made with soap. I didn't know exactly what they meant. I understood it had to do with sex and taking a joint shower. What did they mean? Did he refer to inserting the soap into the vagina? Impossible. I stopped thinking about it.

The morning went by sluggishly. Soon Jonathan would come over, but I still didn't know what I would do. I was reminded of the picture he had sent me. He had a huge penis, thick and long, it was slightly scary. I was startled. I didn't think I could contain it.

I was angry at myself; why was I even thinking about it? After all, I wasn't planning on doing anything with him. But to be on the safe side, I placed the lubricant in my nightstand.

I prepared lunch for me and dinner for Galit and the grandchildren. I rested on the recliner with my feet up, covered in a soft blanket.

I must have fallen asleep. When I woke up, it was 2:30. I fixed my hair and wore light makeup. I noticed that my cheeks were red, and my eyes sparkled. I was in a good mood. I managed to put on some mascara and wore a new flattering powder-blue cashmere sweater and black pants. I prepared the coffee stand with two mugs, plates, and a delicious cake. I turned on the computer and looked for Leonard Cohen songs on YouTube. Leonard's hoarse and velvety voice played from the computer, as his touching lyrics filled the room.

The antique grandfather clock rang three times. It was 3 PM.

I heard a knock on the door and opened the door wide. Jonathan stood outside, holding a bag of chocolatier pralines. He wore a thin Indian-styled shirt, the kind tourists wear in the Caribbean Islands or the Far

East. I regretted wearing a cashmere sweater. It was too hot, but I looked great in it. Underneath it, I had my sexy black pushup bra. It would seem that I had prepared for this forced meeting. We stood at the entrance to the apartment. Jonathan embraced me at length and then kissed me on the cheek.

It appeared, after all, that I was about to cheat on Mike for the first time.

I contemplated. What was about to happen? I wasn't going to initiate a thing. How would I reject him? But I didn't want to reject him. I didn't know how long it would take, but I wanted it to be over. I was uncomfortable knowing I would cheat on Mike. Sexually, Mike had opened all my chakras. I knew that I needed a man, his touch and everything that came with it. And indeed, there was a man here.

Jonathan took off my sweater. "Shosh, aren't you too hot?"

I had nothing on but my sexy bra. Jonathan lost it. He cupped my breasts. "You have gorgeous breasts," he said and kissed my nipples. They became rock hard.

"You have the breast of a young woman," he said, "and pink nipples of a young girl."

He pressed against me. He had a little gut. I was reminded of Mike's smooth belly, his strong and sturdy arms.

Jonathan squeezed me and his giant penis was pointing at me. "Should I wait, or should I go in?" he asked.

"I'll go put some lubricant," I said.

"I don't think you need any, you're very wet."

And then he suddenly penetrated me. At first, I enjoyed the grinding, but he had an endless penis. All of the sudden, I felt pain in my vagina. Serious pain. Jonathan started moving. I hugged him, but it still hurt.

"I want to hear you moan and scream!" he yelled.

I kept quiet. 'I really am going to scream' I thought. 'When will this nightmare be over?'

Suddenly, I screamed in agony. He thought I was enjoying it. Tears ran down my cheeks.

"Shosh, why are you crying?" Jonathan asked.

"I'm crying with joy," I lied.

Jonathan climaxed.

I moved aside. He had an amazing body, a wonderful penis and the butt of a young man. Mike also had firm buttocks, not saggy like most old men. He was very fit.

Jonathan went to take a shower. "Are you coming?" he asked.

I stayed lying in bed. There was a pink blood stain. I wore a robe.

"I'll go make coffee," I said.

He left the shower wrapped in a towel. He hugged me

and whispered: "I want you again, now."

I was startled.

'Oy vey,' I thought in Yiddish.

I gently pushed him away.

Then, I served him his coffee.

"You should get dressed," I said.

"Shosh, I want to see you again. I finished too quickly, and I'm not sure you did at all. I want to hear you moan and scream."

"I can't meet you at home."

"We can go to a hotel, if you want," he said. "When will we meet again?"

"Let's talk over the phone and schedule," I replied.

I wanted him to leave. On the other hand, I was happy that I had been with a man other than Mike.

Shulamit called Jonathan. He said he'd meet her outside a supermarket in Rehovot.

He apologized that he had to leave early.

"Does Shulamit know where you are?" I asked.

"She knows that the project has been launched. But she doesn't know the schedule," Jonathan replied.

'Odd,' I thought to myself. Jonathan finished his coffee and got dressed. We embraced warmly by the door. He left.

The next day, my crotch and vagina hurt. When I sat

for any length of time, I was in pain; this lasted for a month. I was in real pain. I thought of Dostoyevsky's *Crime and Punishment*.

Was this really Shulamit's idea? I hadn't spoken to her about it. Perhaps she said it as a joke, and he took it seriously. And maybe he was tricking me and using the fact that I had come back defeated and heartbroken. I decided this would never happen again. It was unethical.

Shabbat Shalom

Friday had come. I bought challah for Shabbat, candles, a sweet wine for Kiddush, a Cabernet Sauvignon and a Gewürztraminer, a white fruity wine from the Alsace region.

My daughters' friends arrived with their children, Smadar was among them with the twins. We sat and chatted. Shabbat was about to begin. I wore a white handkerchief on my head and blessed the candles. Shabbat created an atmosphere of softness and purity.

Smadar's husband called every now and then to ask when she was coming back so they could go to the mosque together. Smadar kept telling him that she was with her friends and that she would soon come. She wanted to stay with us.

I said Kiddush later. "The heavens and the earth were finished, and all their vast array…" we sliced the challah,

I dipped it in salt, handing it to all those present and blessed the bread. After we ate, I made sure to say the blessing of the food and sing the songs I knew from home. Smadar wore her veil and the twins kept sitting with us. She won't be going to the mosque tonight. I didn't see it as a victory. I couldn't quite figure out Smadar; She was a Jewish Muslim. She missed the traditions and values of her parents' home, but she also loved her husband and his family, who accepted her for who she was. She adopted the Muslim ways. It was hard to argue with that reality. People who were considered enemies became lovers. Eventually, love triumphs all. I didn't want to get into any political arguments with myself or those around me. Such an argument would have no winners or losers. We were riding the wings of history.

I was supposed to go out that evening with a Facebook friend.

We texted several times on Messenger and WhatsApp. The conversation was somewhat telegraphic, and I was disinterested.

"How are you?"

Like.

"What's up?"

Two likes.

"When can we meet?"

"Tonight? Tomorrow?"

"Tonight."

Three likes.

I told myself that I had nothing to expect from such an evening.

He told me that he was a farmer, he owned a big farm up north, not too far from the Sea of Galilee and Mount Hermon. He was going to visit his children and grandchildren in Kfar Saba, and this was also his chance to meet me. He sent me a picture a couple of days ago. He seemed rather sweet. He had dark hair, curls and rather smiley. He was an environmental activist, a scientist, a seed researcher and developer, something that had to do with the Ministry of Agriculture and the Volcani Center, an agricultural research organization.

I told him where I lived and asked that he park next to house number 20. We scheduled for 9 PM.

He called precisely at 9. "I'm waiting for you, why aren't you coming down?"

"I'll be there in five minutes," I replied.

When I came downstairs and looked around, I saw no one. He called again.

"It's been 5 minutes. Where are you?"

"I'm here," I replied.

"I can't see you."

"Where did you park?" I asked.

"I parked next to house number 12."

'Oh wow, what a dumbass,' I thought. "I told you to park next to number 20," I said.

"Right, but I couldn't turn around from number 20."

"So how did you expect to see me next to number 12?"

For some reason it reminded me of the "hole in the bucket" song.

I sat on one of those new benches the municipality had installed on the sidewalk. I couldn't see anyone. There were many passersby. Suddenly, I saw someone waving at me. For a moment, I thought it was a child. That was my date for the night. He was cute, but very short.

We walked for quite some time to his car, which was parked on the nearby street. He held my hand and pulled me, as if we had been friends forever.

'I hope not to be seen by any acquaintances,' I thought. I was rather ashamed to walk beside him.

We sat in the car. "What should we do?" he asked me.

'Why should I decide?' I thought. "You wanted to meet, so come on, let's do what you've planned," I said.

He kept quiet.

I finally suggested, "Let's have some coffee and chat."

"Where?" he asked.

"A café?"

'It's like talking to the wall,' I thought. 'How do I get out of this?'

"Okay, let's go the Kfar Maccabiah Hotel, they have a nice café," he suggested.

"Oh, stop. Kfar Maccabiah Hotel is way out of the city. I have a principle. I'm not traveling with a stranger out of town," I said.

"Why?" he asked.

"If we fight, for instance, how would I get back? I'm dependent on your car. How could I stop a taxi on the highway in the middle of night? Bottom line, it doesn't work for me."

"Why would we fight?" he asked.

"Anything can happen. There's a nice restaurant nearby. Let's sit there," I said.

"Okay," he replied. "I brought you some tomatoes from my greenhouse."

"Thank you."

When we arrived at the restaurant, he ordered fish. This place was known for its delicious sandwiches and steaks. I ordered a California sandwich – it had fried chicken with fresh vegetables, lettuce and mayonnaise – and a cup of coffee. I thought we'd sit together and chat. He swallowed his fish rather quickly and waited for me to finish my sandwich and coffee. In any case, I wasn't in a hurry. I ate my sandwich slowly and took small sips from my coffee. "There's a garden out here. It's nice, there's a good breeze," I said.

I saw that he was impatient. But I didn't really care. I wasn't planning on meeting him for a second date. He said that as part of his job he came to Tel Aviv once a week and slept at the Kfar Maccabiah Hotel. He said he'd like to go steady with me. Next time we meet, he'd like us to spend the night together. I told him that I knew someone who lived in a small village by Rehovot, who owned a horse farm and that I might also meet with him.

"I want to see no one else but you, and you me. Let's go, we'll talk in the car. It's more comfortable there," he said.

I reluctantly stood up. When we reached the car, I asked him, "Okay, tell me about yourself."

Instead of replying he started groping me and shoving his tiny hands down my bra. I can't even remember if he washed his hand after eating that fish. There were people passing by. I was uncomfortable.

An eighty-year-old woman making out with a man in a car in public. After all, I wasn't a fifteen-year-old girl. This was unexpected, too soon and not at all what I wanted.

"You have nice breasts," he said. "You have stunning nipples; I want to suck them."

'What was he thinking?' I thought. 'What an idiot. Me, at my age? Get naked in a car in the middle of the street, just a couple of blocks from my house?'

Suddenly the phone rang. It was his daughter; she was concerned. "Is everything okay, daddy? When are you coming?"

"Soon," he replied.

"Shosh," he said to me anxiously, "let's move to the backseat."

I couldn't believe what I was hearing. The man had lost his mind. Move to the backseat like a high school girl, with my walking cane, and lie in the back? I haven't done that in a long time. And in any case, I wasn't planning on fooling around with him.

We sat in the front seat. He drove off and moved the car to a darker corner. He started thrusting his hands into my sexy underwear and found the engorged spot of my clitoris. He pressed it firmly, because probably, that's what he thought he should do. I pretended to heave.

All of the sudden, I felt a painful scratch. I pulled his hand out, and absentmindedly touched his fingernails. He had a broken nail. He had scratched me in my most intimate area. I deserved it!

He kept sitting there as if nothing had happened and started unzipping his jeans. I looked at them, he must have shopped for them at the kids' department. Now, it was my turn to put my hand in there and rummage around. I thought I'd stumble upon a substantial penis. They say that short people have large dicks. It has to do with an old joke, the kind Alex liked to tell.

It goes like this: when God handed out penises, he hung them on a string. The tall men grabbed the short ones, and the short men grabbed the long ones.

Finally, after searching his genitals, I found a tiny member, rock hard and erect. He looked at me with a puzzled expression. "When will we meet again?" he asked.

I used the best excuse I had, the one that always worked: "Sorry, I can't I have a boyfriend in New York."

"So why did you meet me?" he asked with a somewhat angry tone.

"He sees other women too, I think," I replied.

He drove me home.

"What about the tomatoes?" he asked.

I didn't want to take home anything that would remind me of him and this absurd evening.

"Use them to make a salad for your kids," I said. 'I just want him out of here!' I thought.

Later, I suffered from soreness in my clitoris because of his broken nail. How rude! I was in pain and I couldn't sit down – *again*. Crime and Punishment.

He tried communicating with me again in his special telegraphic way.

"How was it?" and he added two likes.

I didn't respond.

After a few failed attempts, he wrote that he was unfriending me on Facebook.

'Big Deal!' I thought.

A Tale of a Plumber

One of my Facebook friends I talk to almost on a daily basis is a man who lives in Brooklyn. His name is Ehud Bass. He is an Israeli who had been married for over fifty years and had a huge family. He had two children – a daughter who had become religious, and a son, who's a doctor in Iowa. Ehud is more than seventy-years old. About a year ago, he had a partial leg amputation and stayed many months at home, waiting for the right prosthesis. He and his wife live in different wings of the house. Sometimes they would even communicate by phone.

Ehud has dozens of conversations with women on Facebook and friends. Most of the time, his wife is with her best friend or visits their daughter and helps her. She makes him basic meals and hardly takes care of him. She refers to the women he corresponds with as "whores." I once heard the way she spoke to him, bluntly, with a cold and distant voice.

I was on the line, so she blurted: "Are you on the phone with one of your whores again?"

I felt bad that they had that kind of relationship. They lived in a beautiful area in Brooklyn, next to a river and green trees. They had installed an elevator for him, and the house was large and well-kept. His wife had worked at the World Trade Center. After 9/11, the company she had worked for went bankrupt and she lost her job. Ever since, she was in a never-ending nervous breakdown. With a friend of his, Ehud had made a successful investment thirty years before. They had bought an apartment in Manhattan next to the Met, and they were now renting it. Ehud had worked for many years as a taxi driver in New York and had so many stories to tell; how he drove Clinton to a meal at the Plaza Hotel, how he drove different celebrities and well-known actors.

It was important for me to have a friend in New York with whom I did not have any romantic ties. I needed a friend, so that when I flew to New York I wouldn't be dependent on Mike. I wanted to have someone who would show me around the city. I would have been pleased if Ehud and his wife got back together. They had all that it took to have a happy life. Ehud was a very handsome man; he resembled Paul Newman. Perhaps he wasn't telling me the truth and his wife had a different reason to be mad at him. Maybe he had cheated on her in the past. I don't know. But even if he had, now he needed her help and love. I wish they would resolve their issues and live happily by each other's side.

In any case, I kept talking to him. The only problem was that he was a relentless justice seeker. He constantly complained about US and Israeli politics. It was a shame that he couldn't simply enjoy life.

A few days ago, I noticed my toilet was leaking, and it only got worse. The plumber we used to work with had retired and closed his business. I didn't want to call one of those plumbers who left their fliers by the door. Ehud had just called. We spoke of this and that, about medical conditions and medicine, about men and women. We talked about everything. I told him that what I wanted at this very moment was to find a plumber in Tel Aviv.

Ehud laughed and said: "Wait, I'll find you a plumber."

"How would you find me a plumber? You're in New York."

"Hang up and you'll soon get a phone call from a plumber."

"How? Tell me!"

"Shosh, wait and see. It's a surprise!"

Less than five minutes later, my phone rang. Avi the plumber was on the line. He arrived within two hours and fixed the toilet at a reasonable price. I thought this was a nice story; how I got a plumber in the Middle East through a conversation with someone in New York.

"Thank you, Ehud Bass."

My last attempts with men had led to poor results. My vagina hurt. My crotch hurt. My clitoris hurt. I decided to abstain from sex for the foreseeable future. I told Ehud Bass what had happened to me. He laughed.

There's No Life Without Him

Mike would call me twice or more each week. I missed him very much. I started to think that our love was one-sided on my part.

"No matter what, Shosh Kinneret," Mike would say, "you're very dear to me. I have deep feelings for you. I was a close friend of Alex, and I'll forever stay your loyal friend."

Perhaps I wanted to hear more than that, but I was happy to hear from him, nonetheless. Maybe he said those things just to go through the motions. What is the truth? I'll never know.

Mike was preoccupied with what he thought to be his life's mission. The issue was very important to him. I was somewhat of a closure for him. He was also about to receive a significant prize at a cardiology conference that was about to take place in Los Angeles.

I decided to write an email to Sam, Alex's friend who lived in the Dominican Republic, the same friend who introduced me to Igor, also known as Mike Ziv. He's the one who brought us together. I said that I was worried since I hadn't heard from him in over a year. I wanted to know whether he and his wife were feeling well. I told him that Mike was about to receive an important prize and that he should congratulate him personally. Mike would probably be thrilled.

I received a reply from Sam a few days later. He wrote that he was glad I had reached out. They were all doing well. His wife, the children, and the grandchildren in Israel. He, however, was struggling health-wise. After all, he was over 80.

On his next email he wrote that he was sorry to inform me that Mike Ziv had passed away a couple of months before. I was shocked. I had spoken to Mike the other day. I knew he was mistaken. I couldn't understand why Sam was spreading such false information among his friends. He knew that Mike and I were in touch, and that we were about to get married.

Why was he doing it? Was he mad at Mike for some reason?

I knew that in the past, Sam offered Mike some sort of deal, and that he had met him in New York. I also knew that Mike was preoccupied with his research and clinics and refused to tag along on unsafe financial adventures.

In any case, the news shook me. I suddenly felt that if Mike were no longer in this world, something would break inside of me. He must be alive, even if he was with a different woman. The most important thing was for him to be here, for me to be able to speak to him every now and then, and perhaps even touch his hand, feel him. I knew there was something between us that was beyond love, beyond lust, a certain force in the universe, the light in my heart.

The World Will Never Be the Same Without Mike

I suddenly had a better realization of the essence of the bond we shared. I treated it as a mystical matter. As something that extended beyond the physical. And that with my mind alone, I could send him a message. No! I could never live in a world without Mike in it.

I was also very possessive of him. I think he was a true playboy, a womanizer.

Perhaps I'm wrong. Maybe he's just an old man, a lonely widower who wanted to find a spouse with whom he could share his twilight years.

After Mike, none of the men I met satisfied me; physically or spiritually.

I pondered. Should I tell Mike what Sam had written? I didn't want to distract him so close to the conference where he would accept his award. At first, I thought I would contact his son. Eventually, I decided to ignore what Sam had written and not speak a word of it. I didn't reply to his email, I just ignored it. In fact, I stopped writing to him altogether. And yet, to be on the safe side, I told Mike that I had written to Sam about him, and that he had responded inappropriately. Mike said that he wasn't surprised, but he didn't insist that I tell him what Sam had written. Perhaps Mike already knew, and this wasn't the first time that Sam had written such a thing to his friends.

Be that as it may, that email had made things clear for me; Mike must be in this world. As long as I am here, and after that, my love for him only grows. As a matter of fact, it's terrible to love somebody so badly and not have him by your side. It's agonizing. Mike, my love…

A Dream and Its Interpretation

Shulamit called me. I knew she was in recovery from her surgery. Jonathan tried contacting me several times, but I made it clear that what had happened would never repeat itself. Even if this was indeed Shulamit's idea, I wanted none of it. I didn't know whether Shulamit realized what happened with Jonathan, but I sensed that she knew something. She would often browse my Facebook page and try to read between the lines. I was worried that our relationship would be affected by it. After her surgery, Shulamit didn't want anyone's help, she shut herself off and pushed away all her friends. Now, she suggested that she and I take a vacation together. I told her I was planning to travel to the U.S. soon. She suggested that we fly to the Seychelles and spend some time there. Later, I would take a cruise to Miami and meet Mike there, and she would fly back to Israel. I told her I would think about it. I liked the idea of taking a cruise.

I went to sleep. I woke up in the morning with a deja vu sensation about something I couldn't quite define. I had one of those troublesome dreams again; one of those dreams that become clear only many years later.

I was born before WWII. I was a young girl during the war and grew up in Haifa. There were bombings every now and then. I remember that my parents would pull me out of bed and rush me to the nearby shelter. I remembered there were days in which there was much excitement in Israel. The Germans were close to Egypt; too close to us.

One night I went to the bathroom and dreamed with my eyes wide open. There was a big mirror hanging above the sink. In its stead, I saw a big map, probably of Europe. The map was stained in blood. I saw a boot, which represented a footman. I didn't know whether I could recognize the continent. I was just in the second grade. Immediately, as I still sat on the toilet, I felt that I was dreaming again, a short and powerful dream. I sensed pain, and then saw a baby lying by the toilet. It was one of those dreams that one cannot forget.

Later, during the early 60s, when I was in Paris, I got pregnant. I think the baby was Jacques's and not my new boyfriend, Francois', the doctor who took care of me. He inserted a thin tube into my vagina, and it was supposed to abort the pregnancy. Several hours later I felt my uterus contracting. I sat on the bidet. The fetus, which was six centimeters long, fell into the bidet.

I was reminded of that dream!

Once, I was on a cruise that stopped at Port Sa'id in Egypt. When we drove to Cairo, on the way to the pyramids and the Sphinx, I had a sense of deja vu, as if I had been there before. The climate wasn't strange to me, neither were the buildings around us. But that's all it was. I remembered modern buildings, so I probably hadn't been there in an ancient time. I didn't sense that on any of my other trips, not to Greece, France, or the States.

There was yet another dream I often had, a tangible one. The dream took me all the way to biblical times. I was in the heart of the desert, covered in clothes from head to toe. I remember wearing a black dress adorned with two wide red stripes that were sewn into the garment. I was barefoot. I ran as fast as I could with a baby wrapped in rags in my arms. There was no one around. I was so terrified; horrified. I didn't know who I was. I felt it was me, but I didn't know who that woman was. I could have been anyone in the world. Perhaps I was Hagar, running away with her son, Ishmael, and Sarah had just banished us from the tent.

Anything is possible in previous lives, if only one believes it. Perhaps I was a slave woman who had been expelled from her master's house. Perhaps I was running away from some enemy. Perhaps I was a noblewoman from one of the tribes at war, and the baby was the heir. And perhaps this had all happened during those 40 years in which the Israelites walked through the desert, and I, a simple woman, was running from the Amalekites.

I was terrified. I was mostly concerned for the baby, who appeared in many of my dreams.

God! I love you so much, Mike, my old man. I miss you so much.

In fact, it was you, Mike, you threw me out! You think you are the King of England and I am nothing but dust at your feet.

A Million Dollars for a Hug

I was reminded of yet another story from my childhood.

When I was eight years old, I had a brother at the Ezra hospital in Haifa. My dad took me to visit my mom and the baby. Dad said he was born four kilos, and that was wonderful. He was a beautiful baby. He had blonde hair. The color of his eyes was still obscure. My mom wanted to call him Roger, which was a common French name in our family. One day, I wanted to go visit the baby. My parents were very sad. Our pediatrician, a German doctor who lived in the neighborhood, visited us at home. It turned out that the baby had suddenly died.

I didn't buy it. I think I have a brother and he's out there, somewhere. I would have liked to meet him. That is one of my dreams. Perhaps he doesn't know he is adopted, otherwise he would have tried to find his biological family.

Recently, the media had been writing quite a lot about aliyah from the USSR. My Alex was a famous aliyah activist, one of the journalists on TV decided to interview me on one of their panels. We spoke of Alex, of his activity, and how much we all missed him. We spoke of immigrants, and of how they were accepted by and integrated into Israel. We discussed how one leaves an entire life behind and starts a new one in a strange faraway, distant land. I told them I was writing a story about love. I spoke of Alex, my wonderful husband, of Igor, my lover today, both of them Holocaust children, a Holocaust running through great Russia, from one war front to the other. Sadly, Alex is gone.

I remember one day long ago, a journalist from the Jerusalem Post called us looking for Alex. He said that a parliamentary delegation had arrived from Germany and that the head of the delegation wanted to meet Alex. We met him that evening at a hotel in Ramat Aviv. Alex immediately recognized the head of the delegation. At the end of the war, Alex, who was a senior officer in the Red Army, was in charge of the German prisoners in Berlin, and it turned out that the head of the delegation was one of those prisoners. Alex would have lengthy discussions with him, and one day, as Alex strolled the streets of Berlin, he found an ancient bookstore. He noticed a poetry book by Schiller. He purchased it and gave it to his German prisoner. After all that had happened during the war, it was a symbol of grace. Alex proved to be a wonderful humanist; he didn't feel any resentment or a sense of revenge.

I remember all this, as well as the friendship that grew between Alex and Igor.

I loved Alex so much. Now I love Igor, perhaps one-sidedly. I couldn't understand or explain to myself why my love for him was so strong, so overwhelming. Sometimes, I couldn't tell which was better; being with him or missing him and crying my eyes out. If I had a million dollars, I'd give it all away just for a hug with Igor.

The "Million dollars for a hug" thing, had turned into a catch phrase here.

A couple of days ago, I was contacted by an American company representative who liked the gimmick and wanted to do something with it. We are still negotiating with them.

*

I didn't have time to think about sex these last few days. My last experiences were rather bad. I was busy with other things.

One of my Facebook friends contacted me. He called me one night at 2 AM, while I was writing. I answered him just as I was planning to take a break and rest. We started corresponding. Later, he stopped writing back. Suddenly, he called me through Messenger. A picture of him as a young soldier popped up on Facebook. I took the call and a small video screen opened. I saw him. He was lying in bed, covered in a blanket, a sixty-year-old balding man. I was still sitting in front of my computer. He saw that I was up.

"Aren't you in bed at this time?" he asked.

"No, I'm working on something. I just took a coffee break," I replied.

"So, get into bed and let's talk."

I hate when I'm told what to do. I saw he was smiling, slightly bald and round.

"You don't look like your picture," I said.

"Well," he blurted, "it's been quite a few years."

I was rather tired, so I took my clothes off and slipped into my bed under the duvet.

"What are you wearing?" he asked.

I wanted to play coy. "Shalimar!"

"Oh, you're 'wearing' your perfume. Like Marilyn Monroe, do you go to bed with Chanel 5?"

"If you like," I said.

"I want to see your breasts, please, show me…"

'*Haibt zich on a ma'aise*[1]' I thought to myself in Yiddish. I heard him panting. I saw that he was naked and holding on to his member.

"Show me yours. I want to come over tomorrow. I live in Rishon, but I can come to Tel Aviv. Do you have some Viagra?"

"Why would I have any Viagra?"

"I want to cum three times tomorrow. Please, please, please."

I closed the video and hung up.

'Rude! Please, please, like a little child' I thought. It's best to be abstinent if this is what it looks like. Cheap and promiscuous, emotionless. Having sex without a shred of intellect isn't for me. Cheapening sex, that's what it is! 'Sometimes elderly people act like children' I thought.

***

The next day I went to donate bone marrow for a little girl who had cancer.

There was a story in the papers a couple of months ago, about a girl from a settlement by the 1967 Border who had a violent type of Leukemia. The article said that

---

1   Here we go again.

she was in desperate need of a bone marrow donation. There were several stations placed around the country to find a matching donor. One of these stations was by the Tel Aviv Cinematheque. I happened to pass by the area. I walked in and they took a blood sample. I seemed to have forgotten about it. One day they called and told me that my sample matched hers. I asked whether my age should be taken into consideration. They said that it didn't matter and scheduled a time for me to come so they could collect the donation.

Naturally, I gave up on the Viagra fuck and drove to the Petach Tikva to Beilinson hospital. As I laid in bed with an IV painfully stuck in my arm, I thought of Mike; I teared up with joy.

South to Eilat – Shmuel

I'd been called several times by a company that organized vacations in Eilat for senior citizens. These retreats
were also meant to teach the elderly how to use different
digital devices such as smartphones and creating online
blogs. The deal seemed rather attractive. I signed up.
There was only one issue: transportation. Since they
closed the small Sde Dov Airport, it was decided that
we travel by bus, and stop in different locations along the
way, such as an olive oil distillery and a private boutique
vineyard. The bus started its course up north and had a
pickup point in Tel Aviv at the University train station.
I joined a private car that picked me up from home, and
of course, chipped in for gas. We drove behind the bus
and visited all the stops that were planned along the way.
We finally arrived at the Almog beach hotel, about five
kilometers from the city of Eilat.

I noticed that most of the people registered for the trip were women. There were seven women for each man there. The men were ecstatic. I decided to ignore their presence, especially since none interested me. Some were bald, fat, thin, had black or gray hair, and most had a gut. None of them made my nipples perky.

I decided I'd go with the flow, have a good time and rest. I would tan, go to the spa and not lift a finger; I'd leave the hunting to the other women.

I went to sit on the ledge of the swimming pool with some papers and a drink. Suddenly, I noticed a pair of eyes gazing at me. I slowly lifted my head from the paper. The sun blinded me. I noticed a man sitting on the chaise longue in front of me, across the other side of the pool. He seemed tall, had brown hair and some chest curls. He wasn't a member of our group.

In the evening, I wore a light white cotton dress with spaghetti straps. My skin was tan. I felt wonderful. After dinner, I went to sit at a distant corner of the hotel lobby. The group went to see a show. I wasn't interested.

As I sat, someone stood behind me and asked whether the seat next to me was taken. I turned my head and saw the man from the pool with a large smile spread on his face.

"It's free," I said.

He sat quietly, maintaining the silence.

"What's your name?" he asked suddenly.

"Shosh," I said. "And yours?"

"Shmuel."

'Oh goodie,' I thought. 'Shmuel is so soft and smooth. He's the man of my dreams.'

"Are you with a group?" I asked.

"No," he replied. "I'm a contractor from Ashdod. I'm here on business. I came here to have lunch and dinner. I own a yacht in the marina. I might sleep there, or I'll get a hotel room. Can I invite you on a cruise?"

"Thank you, but I came here to rest and tan," I said.

"If you'd like, we don't have to take a cruise. We can sit on the deck with some salmon and champagne. That's what I have to offer."

I sighed.

"On second thought, Shosh, let's go dancing in the club and then go to the yacht."

"Good idea," I said.

The D.J. at the club played light music from the 60s. I ordered a cocktail and Shmuel had some soda since he was driving. After the drinks arrived, we got up to dance. Shmuel pressed me gently against his body. His skin was pleasant to the touch. I felt attracted to him. We kept dancing without saying a word. I didn't feel like having complex conversations, nor did I want to ask him personal questions about him or his family. All I cared about in that moment was to be in his arms. For the first time in a while, I wasn't thinking about Mike.

Shmuel's car was parked at the hotel parking. It was a large and comfortable American car. Shmuel drove swiftly to the marina. The yacht was docked pretty close by. Shmuel sat me on the deck overseeing the sea. In the distance, we saw the lights of Aqaba.

"I'll get us something to eat," he said. "I'll be right back."

Shmuel came back with toast, sliced salmon, lemon and coffee. We ate quietly as we looked at the waves and enjoyed the breeze of the Eilat bay. I heard light jazz music coming from one of the nearby yachts. Shmuel reached out his hand and invited me to dance. I felt good in his arms. I placed my head on his wide shoulder. We danced close to each other. We lusted for each other. Shmuel was the type of man I had fantasized about. A soft and strong body. Curls on his chest. I hate men who remove their chest hair. I felt his penis hardening in his pants. He pulled me off the deck. We walked in the yacht rooms. He took me straight to his sleeping cabin. On the small table by the foot of the large and comfortable bed there was a champagne glass that Shmuel filled from a bottle he'd pulled out of the mini fridge. I sipped from it. Shmuel delicately unbuttoned my cotton dress. I wasn't wearing a bra. Everything went by slowly, but we couldn't hold ourselves any longer. I wasn't thinking of anything. I wanted him so badly. It all happened so fast. Shmuel's soft body squeezed against mine. He caressed my breasts, kissed the curve down my spine and spun me all around. I was burning, completely on fire. His body was hot. I was entirely wet. Shmuel penetrated my vagina from behind. I was in doggy style position. I could enjoy the pleasure of his member thrusting all the way in. He was a perfect match for my cervix, as if he had been molded to fit every fold of my body. With one hand he pressed my clitoris. I had multiple orgasms, and then had a female ejaculation. That hadn't happened in a long time.

"Shmuel!" I called his name as I moaned with pleasure.

He smiled at me, overjoyed. We climaxed together. "You're such a cougar, a lioness and I am your loyal lion" he said.

I'd only just noticed that Shmuel was a relatively young man, in his fifties. I decided that I wouldn't mention my age on this vacation, unless asked.

"Let's go to sleep," he said, and embraced me.

"Okay, let's sleep. And in the morning, you'll take me back to the hotel before breakfast," I said.

I quickly fell asleep between his arms, not one thought about Mike crossing my mind.

In the morning, Shmuel took me back to the hotel.

"Shosh, I'd like to see you again," he said.

"I'm flying to New York in a week."

"I'll join you. I have a few real estate businesses there."

I didn't want to use my usual excuse 'I have a boyfriend in New York' so I kept quiet.

"I'll stay there for about two months," I said. "I'm much older than you are," I told him eventually.

"Age is just a number, my dear, Shosh. You're good for me. We're good for each other. Let's stay in touch. Don't forget me!" Shmuel said.

After breakfast, I took a taxi to Eilat's mall, to do a rather odd thing. I went into a tattoo parlor and asked to have one. I was lying on the bed with a cup of diet Coke, while the tattoo artist tattooed the names of the two men in my life on my shaved pussy. Alex and Mike, in a shape of a heart. It also included my first boyfriend's name, Meir Ziv, who was a Machine Engineering student at the Technion. When I was nineteen, he deflowered me. I didn't care for Jacques, Francois, Shimon, Fima, Joshua, Leon and the others.

Where Is God? Is There a God?

I wanted to write about things that kept me busy, things that crossed my mind from time to time.

The 1755, an earthquake in Lisbon rattled author and philosopher Voltaire, who was, by the way, considered to be anti-Semitic, like many others of his time. He was angry with God who had allowed the earthquake to kill so many innocent people. At a careless moment of whimsy, he said: "There is no God, but don't tell that to my servant, lest he murder me at night." During his outburst at God, Voltaire said, "The universe confounds me! I cannot imagine how the clockwork of the universe can exist without a clockmaker"

And my contemporary words: "If there's an apartment building, where's the housing committee?"

I'm very mad at God for allowing the Holocaust to happen, for slaughtering young babes, women and elderly people who were murdered in the pits and concentration camps, by gas and in the crematoriums. If we were to apply Einstein's relativity theory about time traveling, it would seem that the Holocaust would always take place, and so would the Spanish Inquisition, the Hannibal wars, but also moments of joy, all the way back to the first man. And then perhaps, Eve would have bitten from the Tree of Life and not the Tree of Knowledge?

I'm also angry at the fact that animals are shipped, under terrible conditions, in cargo all over the world, from far away Australia and New Zealand, and when they arrive, after their tedious and terrifying journey, they are taken straight to the slaughterhouse. I eat steak and suffer pangs of remorse.

I think that the particle accelerator in Geneva is harmful to Earth, and now they're planning on building a new one, bigger, stronger, faster.

I'm so angry that we know so little, or nothing at all, about the essence of human existence, on the lack of meaning regarding our existence on Earth. We have no control over our fate, we are a part of a system. Even if we do believe in reincarnation, our next life is always geographically close and takes place in the same regions. We have no control of our future. We are cogs, screws, springs in the system. We are placed on Earth within this family or that. Go figure, good or bad. There's a crime and a punishment, and sometimes, there's nothing more but a crime, without any punishment.

I dreamed about Dali's clock painting, The Persistence of Memory; Mike and I were running on the clock's numbers. He was running, I was being strung along. I was trying to keep up but failed. That was the last straw. As if we were running on two parallel lines, without a meeting point. Today, at the age of eighty-two, I wasn't cut out to be someone's wife. Do the cleaning and cooking, prepare rich gourmet meals, Shabbat and holiday dinners, having guests and family over, my family and his, and above all – playing the role of the perfect woman. Plus, I couldn't stand for a long time during ceremonies, listen to lectures and promises, shake hands of dozens of honorable yet unimportant people who happened to be there.

I'm not the Queen of England. I don't want to get married.

I want a free partner, a man to my liking who can offer me pleasure and financial stability. Someone I'd have a good time with, who wouldn't inspect my every move. I won't prepare gourmet meals for him... maybe occasionally, if I felt like it.

But if, God forbid, he'd be sick, I'd take him to the

doctor and be there for him, I'd care for him and nurse him.

I love going out with Mike to a restaurant or an outing or a short walk, I love spending time in bed with him, feeling him, hugging him, kissing and loving him endlessly.

Sometimes, I think of all the men I have known in my life. Most of them have already passed away, one of them had one of the most senior positions in the country. I can't talk about him because he is no longer with us.

Sometimes, I google the men I've known. Some have excelled in their fields, and others have reached rock bottom and are now on welfare. They live and die in different places around the world.

May they rest in peace.

The Seychelles

Shulamit called me again. "What do you think of my offer? Us going together on a vacation to the Seychelles? You need to recover from your adventure in New York and I need to recover from my surgery."

"Aren't you taking a vacation with Jonathan?" I asked.

"Not this time. I want to go with a friend. A girl's trip."

"No men?" I asked.

"I didn't say that," she said, as if in secret. "There are men there. We'll have them if we want."

"Okay, Shulamit. Gladly. Organize it as you like, and I'll adjust my schedule accordingly."

I wondered whether Shulamit knew what had truly happened between Jonathan and me. I think he eventually confessed. He didn't hide anything from her. Should I talk to her about it? Perhaps that subject was taboo, or would it come up on our vacation?

I didn't want to talk about it. Shulamit was my best friend. We spoke to each other about everything, but as a scientist she shied from empty gossip. I know that when I was in New York I wanted to pour my heart out and was met with a brick wall. I wanted her encouragement and advice, but she wouldn't give it. I felt the loneliness strike me at its hardest. I couldn't talk about it with my daughter, Galit, either. She would tell me defiantly: "I told you so! He dumped you! He's an egotistical stubborn man who loves no one but himself."

I thought about my vacation with Shulamit, of how we would stare silently at the waves, the coconut and palm trees.

She would think about her polymers and whatever she had in her petri dishes, and my thoughts would sail away to Mike, of how much I wanted him to be there by my side, among all the blues and turquoises. My spirit cries out for him, while he might be messing around in New York with some Ukrainian guest or cute woman who's making him Russian Shabbat meals against a backdrop of fake roses and an impressive Faberge Egg collection.

Perhaps I'll take some local lover boy in the Seychelles, someone who'll take me to different places and dance with me without us sleeping together. I couldn't understand why Shulamit chose to go with me and not

Jonathan. Maybe she wanted, while staying in those paradisiacal islands, to calmly hear what really happened between Jonathan and me, if at all? But for that we could also sit at a café in Tel Aviv; we didn't have to waste five thousand dollars to travel to the Seychelles. While I am indeed a wealthy woman, that is not a sum so easily spent.

We visited the island that had the most beautiful beach in the world; the La Digue Island. The locals took great care of the environment. They claimed that we must preserve nature as we are only temporary guests, and it must be honored.

The Seychelles are located in the Indian Ocean, facing East Africa, south of the Arabian Peninsula, about a six-hour flight from Israel. Tropical islands, forests, jungles, peace, white beaches, clear water in different shades of turquoise. It's a desirable location, a heaven on earth. They have some of the most beautiful nature reserves in the world. The government prohibits building structures that are taller than the highest coconut trees. It is, in fact, an archipelago comprised of five groups of central islands, 155 islands in total. People use shuttles to travel throughout the islands. The central island, Mahé, is the most populated and largest island. The capital is Victoria and it is located three kilometers from the international airport. The languages are Creole (a French-African dialect), French and English. Vallée de Mai Nature Reserve in itself, and it where the coco de mer is grown. It had become the symbol of Seychelles, as the male and female coconuts resemble male and female genitalia. Our hotel was a grouping of luxurious bungalows, spread apart from one another. Each bungalow had a private swimming pool that merged with the sea and the green trees.

We drank fruit-based cocktails in abundance. Much to my surprise, Shulamit started talking about sex. She asked me what I thought of Jonathan. I knew from her stories that he had a large penis, so I told her that if I were to actually handle it, I probably would not be able to sit down for a month. She burst out laughing.

On our second evening in La Digue, I wore a light blue cotton dress with spaghetti straps. I was pretty tanned from our long stay by the ocean. I headed to Shulamit's bungalow.

We booked two private bungalows. I could have booked one for the both of us, but we preferred the freedom and privacy. Shulamit's bungalow was lit with artificial oil lamps, and the sun began to set outside. It was one of the most beautiful sunsets I had ever seen. The white curtains in the bungalow blew with the ocean breeze. Suddenly, I noticed two men standing under the pale bungalow light. Shulamit had a sly smile on her face. They were two dark and tall men, with dark colored curls and chiseled faces. They looked like two Roman gods. They each wore jeans and a matching leather belt, a thin cotton shirt, partially unbuttoned, and they wore strap sandals. They seemed to be in their late thirties, or early forties.

"Shosh, dear, come meet Pierre and Claude. They speak French and English."

"Good, Shulamit. What do you intend to do with them?" I asked in Hebrew, of course.

"Shosh, they're ours for the night, we can do whatever the hell we want, okay?"

"Wait, we need to pay them, Shulamit?"

"Don't worry, Shosh, I already paid them."

"You should know that on principle I do *not* pay for sex!"

"Shosh, if it appeases your conscience, treat it like an anthropological experiment."

"Shulamit, you're forgetting that you're almost twenty years younger than me. We don't see things the same way."

"That much I know," she added, throwing yet another poisonous dart at me. "Come on, Shosh, join us and let's go to dinner. Then we'll go dancing at the hotel club. And later, who knows?"

'What's with Shulamit? She never says such things. I rather like it,' I thought.

"Shulamit, who's taking whom?" I asked.

"I'll take Pierre and you take Claude. Does that work for you?"

"I find them both yummy, so I don't mind."

We ate in a pastoral atmosphere by windows over-looking the ocean. We had Creole cuisine. There was a huge buffet that included a variety of: chicken, fish and seafood, shrimps and clams, vegetables, sauces, and for dessert – tropical fruits. We were served French wine to quench our thirst. We savored the rich food.

Our escorts went to the buffet and came back with packed plates. A pleasant tune was playing. Shulamit took Pierre to the dance floor. Claude and I looked at them. After a couple of dances, I saw Shulamit disap-pearing with Pierre, both lazily heading to her bunga-low. I was slightly shocked. Shulamit, my best friend, was sleeping around. I stayed with Claude. I knew he was rented for the night. I had never paid for sex or, as Shulamit put it with a smidge of condescension, anthro-pological research.

I didn't know what I'd do with Claude. I didn't know what to say to him. He should rack his own brains. Perhaps I should dismiss him?

I looked at him. He was a handsome man, as beautiful as Michelangelo's David, sculpted during the Renaissance and placed in Florence. I wanted to dismiss him, but how could I let such a beautiful thing go?

I was under the impression that he was having fun and wanted to say. I spoke to him in French. When I looked at him, I thought of Mike. What wouldn't I give to be with Mike at that moment? I preferred Mike over him.

Claude looked at me and asked, "Why are you sad?"

"Sometimes, things in life make you sad, and you don't even know why," I replied. "I may go to sleep early, so you can leave."

"Let me pay you back," Claude said.

"No need," I replied. "The money is yours. Let's not talk about it anymore. I'm sorry, I'm tired."

"Let's sit on the seashore and you'll rest as much as you like. I won't bother you, I'll just sit by your side," Claude said. "You're a fascinating woman. I want to stay with you."

He brought towels, pillows and a light blanket. He then spread it on the white sand, close to the water.

I took my sandals off and sprawled on the towel. He

lay beside me and caressed my hair. I rested my head on his broad shoulder. We lay there for a long time, as the Indian Ocean tide tickled our toes.

I miss my old, charming, noble Mike.

A couple of days of fun and walks throughout the islands had passed. I met with Claude, but he refused to take my money.

Shulamit was supposed to fly back to Israel and I waited for a luxury cruise ship that would take me to Miami. Mike called and asked how things were going. I notified him of my plans. He promised he would wait for me at the Miami dock.

On the morning of the cruise, Claude came to my bungalow to say goodbye. We chatted, hugged and discussed his plans. He was a wonderful painter. His paintings were colorful and reminded me of Paul Gauguin's work. I suggested that he focus on his paintings and sell them to tourists and leave his escorting career behind, at least for the most part. He smiled.

"I love meeting all kinds of women, it's so interesting," he said. He handed me a note with his phone number. Another hug, and then Claude was gone. I put the note in my pocket. I placed the pants on the chair by my robe and went to take a shower. I didn't notice that the note had slipped out and fell into the shower. I began to bathe and thought of Mike. The water dampened the note and some of the number was smudged. It was too late when I noticed it. 'Oh well,' I thought to myself, 'I won't visit this part of the world again.'

Veni, Vidi, Vici

When I was still in New York, during my deliberation period, I sat by the breakfast table. I washed the dishes and poured myself another cup of coffee. Mike sat on the stairs, wore socks and sneakers, like a little boy. My heart went out to him. He wore his perennial black cap, pecked my cheek and left for work. I sat with my phone, ready to start a round of calls.

I called my daughter from the American phone Mike had given me. It was his wife's phone. My grandchildren wanted to see the presents I had bought them. We had a video call and I showed them their gifts. I bought Alon several types of Beyblades, cars, a chess boardgame, and an impressive Nerf gun. Alon said that he didn't like guns; I was pleased to hear it.

I got Ilanit a mermaid Barbie with a shiny twirling tail. She asked if this was The Little Mermaid, Ariel. I replied that it was.

The children were very pleased.

A couple of minutes later I heard the Israeli phone ring. I didn't quite understand how, because I hadn't opened the line to international calls. It was the Chabad rabbi who worked at the rabbinate in Tel Aviv. Perhaps he was speaking from New York. He asked about the wedding. I explained that it was no longer relevant since I had pneumonia, and I have a leg problem, as well as a severe toe wound. I asked him about the marriage file we had opened. He said that if we weren't getting married, we should close it, otherwise, we wouldn't be able to marry other people should we choose to. I told him I'd speak to Mike. I also decided to ask about the procedure for canceling our registration. He replied that both spouses need to arrive at the rabbinate and sign.

"If Mike doesn't come to Israel, can we do it by courier?" I asked. The rabbi avoided the question and replied that we must sign there. I told him I would talk to Mike about it.

When Mike came back, I told him about the conversation with the rabbi.

"Let's leave it," he replied.

"The way it is? Opened?" I asked.

"Yes, Shosh. Opened!"

Once again, he was forcing his thoughts on me.

I looked at him glumly, and at the same time, I was overcome with a desire to be held in his arms; he could keep talking, all I wanted was to hear his ringing, hoarse voice.

'What kind of love was this?' I thought to myself. 'Will it last forever? Or will it gradually fade?'

I went up to the bedroom. Mike followed me. I wanted to say, at least this once, that I was tired. But all my chakras opened up the moment he touched me, we melted into each other, I moaned and briefly forgot that the cleaner was working in the other wing of the house. But why should I care? I'm leaving anyway. I kept screaming, but Mike was alarmed and placed a finger on my lips, trying to keep me quiet.

I laughed. "Mike, I'm leaving in a couple of days, and that's that."

"Shosh, you're leaving, and I'll come to visit. We're just taking a break," Mike said. "Come, silly." He collected me in his arms. We kissed in length. I felt his penis harden again.

I was lying back on a couple of pillows. I was nearly naked, aside from a thin short crop top that covered my nipples. "Next time don't wear anything at all," he whispered. His penis was erect, pointing at the ceiling. Suddenly, I gently sat up and casually sat on it and his penis penetrated my wet vagina. We stayed there for a couple of minutes, still, vibrating and sweating. I felt him climaxing with me. I leaned over him and covered his penis with my mouth, despite the wetness. I chose to do it. I wouldn't do it for anyone else in the world, aside from Alex. I gently licked his balls, trying to lightly swallow them.

'Now I can go home,' I thought. **Veni, Vidi, Vici**[2], as Julius Caesar would say.

---

2   I came, I saw, I conquered

"Sh'ma Yisrael Adonai Eloheinu Adonai Ehad!"[3]

There were two luxury cruises to Miami that docked in the Seychelles. One was longer than the other and it sailed through Thailand, India, the Japanese Islands, Hawaii, entered America through the Panama Canal, and then to Miami. I chose the short route via the African coast.

I waited in Mahé Island to embark on the cruise ship. I stayed at a hotel in the capital of Victoria. I sat on the white beach as my eyes drowned in the turquoise shades of the Indian Ocean waters. I was reminded of how I had sat on the porch of the villa in the south of France, close to San Tropez, my eyes ravished for the blue shades of the navy colored waters. That was during the period I worked at the Israeli Tourism office in Paris, at the

---

3   "Hear, O Israel: the LORD our God, the LORD is one!"

beginning of the sixties. I was reminded of how the bureau manager approached me one day and invited me to his office. He told me that the Israeli Aerial Attaché had been looking for me because they had an offer for me. That meant I had to take a couple of months off, and if I agreed, someone from the Military Attaché at the Israeli Embassy would come to speak with me. I asked if he approved that I take this time off. The bureau manager, Yaakov, told me that he didn't have a problem with such priorities. I told him I'd need to hear about the position before I made up my mind.

During those times there wasn't yet a weapons embargo between France and Israel. Israeli pilots trained in Israel and at French air bases, flying the *Mystère* and *Ouragan*.

The next day, someone from the military attaché office called, and we scheduled to meet at the tourism bureau.

We had a pleasant conversation. He told me that he couldn't provide details about the position. He could only tell me that I would have to travel to the French Riviera and live there in a villa in the heart of the forest. There would be two Israeli servants living in the villa with me and attending to the household. Sometimes, they would host dinners for guests and friends; about thirty people. There would be a catering service that would take care of the food, beverages and the service. I would have at my disposal a white Maserati GT. I would have to drive each day to San Tropez and sit by the marina with an easel as I paint. I can have coffee and sit in different restaurants on the boardwalk. I would have a stipend and an expense account; I would earn double the salary I did at the Tourism Bureau. It sounded magical and had an air of mystery. Naturally, I agreed.

I was given a week to prepare. I loved to paint. I bought some canvases and exquisite oil paints in rich blues and reds, all shades of cyan and turquoise, different hues of green and magenta. Three days later, I was already on the Blue Train to the Riviera. A driver waited for me at the train station, and he drove me to the villa that was located in the middle of a forest, overlooking a blue sea view. It was wonderful.

I was slightly afraid to live in the forest, because of the occasional fires. But the rest of it was fascinating. I was the lady of the villa. The next day, I loaded my painting equipment and drove to San Tropez in my Maserati. I bought a yuppie wardrobe in advance in some boutique stores on the boardwalk. Clothing that would suit my stature, the region and season.

I looked for a comfortable location to place my easel. The next day I would start painting.

A week later, there were twenty-people for dinner at the villa. The caterers prepared a summer Provence meal: fish, sea food, salads and fresh fruits. We mostly drank rosé wine. Most of the guests were Israeli pilots who trained nearby.

My life in the villa went by sluggishly. I sat so much in the marina that my skin had a golden tan. The San Tropez port manager began to show an interest in my paintings. I could paint well and loved working with oil colors. I gradually got to know the locals and the business owners who worked during the summer tourist season. In the winter, they would close their businesses and rest, or keep working at the famous French ski resorts.

One night, it seemed that the forest had come to life. I heard explosions, screams and a commotion. I'm sure I heard a weapon being fired. The couple who tended to the household quickly ran outside and came back with a young man who had a bullet wound in his shoulder. They laid him in one of the guest rooms. I got up and wanted to call a doctor. The housekeeper's husband re-assured me that he would take care of it. He injected the shoulder of the wounded man, who spoke Hebrew, with local anesthesia and managed to extract the bullet.

The next day after breakfast I went to the wounded man's room. I knocked on the door and walked in. He had just finished eating. I took his tray and placed it on the table. I sat by his bed and asked if there was anything else that he needed.

"There's nothing else I need, but please, don't leave. Come, sit with me," he replied.

I stayed there. I knew that I couldn't ask him any personal questions, or any inquiries that pertained to what had happened the night before.

If he wanted to tell me, then he would. In this type of position, the less you know, the better. I smiled at him. He was a nice young man, about twenty-seven years old, kind, handsome and blue-eyed, just the way I liked it.

I visited him every morning after breakfast. I sat down and we spoke for about half an hour. Then I would leave to paint in San Tropez. At nights he would watch TV, read newspapers and do his crosswords.

One morning, he asked that I stay a little longer. He said that in a couple of days he would be leaving.

"Shoshana," he said, "I like you a lot."

"I think it's mutual," I said.

He kissed me softly.

"Come back at night. I'll be dreaming of you until you do," he said.

I shook his hand and kissed him lightly in response.

"I don't even know your name," I said.

"My name is Arik and I'm a pilot."

"My name is Shosh and I'm a painter," I reply in a similar manner.

He winked back.

I drove to San Tropez and looked for new painting location. I walked to the lighthouse and sat there. The port manager suddenly appeared. 'How did he find me? Was he following me?' I thought.

He sat next to me and smiled sympathetically. "I see you almost every day. I was thinking to myself what such a beautiful woman is doing walking around on her own."

I told him, "*Il vaut mieux être seule que mal accompagné*" – it is better to be alone than to have bad company.

He smiled and said that a little boat had docked at the port an hour before, with two young men who had caught a large shark. They were looking for people to join them – they were sailing into the ocean in a couple of hours. "Let's go there," he said.

We walked to the small boat that docked in the marina. There was quite a commotion on the boat; two muscular young men were holding long knives and were about to gut the shark to see what it had swallowed. I noticed that the shark was still alive, it moved its fins and its expressionless eyes moved. I preferred avoiding that sight.

"Would you like to join them?" the port manager asked.

I sarcastically smiled at him to 'get out of my sight!' and walked off the boat and waved goodbye. There was no point in fighting with the authorities.

The sun began to marvelously set and was swallowed by the horizon, which, in turn became silver. Evening fell.

I sat on the porch at the front of the villa. I had dinner and sipped some cool Chardonnay. I basked in all that beauty. I would soon rest. It was midnight. I wore a thin cotton robe on top of my sexy lingerie.

After I ate, I went to Arik's room. I saw him standing in his jeans and his bare chest had a small patch of curly hair. His shoulder was bandaged. 'How wonderful' I thought 'he doesn't have a bare chest'. He held two glasses of champagne. I approached and embraced him. I took one of the champagne glasses from his hand. We slowly drank that bubbly wine in small sips.

"Shosh, if you'd like, we can travel tomorrow to Nice and eat at the officers' club," he said.

"Okay, as you wish," I replied.

We placed the champagne glasses on the table. Arik refilled the crystal flutes. We hugged. The scent of his skin reminded me of the Israeli sun and fragrant orchards. It was odd how pleasant it was to be reminded of Israel in a foreign country. I had suddenly become somewhat of a Zionist. I hugged him and felt that I was melting. He symbolized Israel to me. It even seemed that the air I breathed was spicier and tingly. As if I was breathing him and the scent of Israel in. He was a field of anemones, a rock in the Judean Mountains, a shield of gold against the walls of Jerusalem. Though he had only stayed in the room these last few days, his body was still tanned to a copper shade. I couldn't help myself and held him tightly. He took off my robe. I stayed in my lingerie. He took off his jeans. To my surprise, he wasn't wearing any underwear. He turned his back to me and walked to bed. I looked at him and his back, a triangle of long, gentle muscles. He had an amazingly firm butt. Arik slipped under the white sheet, turned around and smiled at me. I unhooked my bra and sat on the bed. He lay down and waited.

"Shosh, I want you to stay the whole night with me," he said.

He moved the sheet aside. I saw his dick: beautiful, erect like a spear. He tucked his hand into my underwear. He slowly removed it and touched me. I was so wet. He didn't say a word, which was for the best. The night became pitch black. We hugged again. My vagina yearned for his touch. His penis looked for my genitals in the darkness. We were both wild animals, two beasts craving one another. He found the cave and moaned as he penetrated me. "I feel like I'm swimming in a lake, Shosh. I'm drowning in delight," he said. "My dear, come to me every night and I will give you a child." And so I did. I wanted him so much. I would follow him to the ends of earth. I stayed in his bed until morning. The housekeeper served us our breakfasts.

I knew he had to leave. He didn't go into detail and I didn't ask any questions.

On our last night together, he told me that he was going back to the field. "It's dangerous," he said. "I can't tell you more than that. I love you. Pray for me. Wait for me."

I prayed every evening after he left and said the Sh'ma Israel prayer.

With my breakfast I would receive Hebrew newspapers – *Ha'aretz*," *Ma'ariv*," *Yediot Aharonot* and *The Jerusalem Post*.

One morning they didn't bring any papers. People walked around the villa with a solemn expression. They served my breakfast and quickly left. I later found out that the whole country was completely stirred: an Israeli pilot whose plane crashed in Jordan was captured by Palestinians who lynched him. They used his dental records to identify the body.

Cleaning Out the Stables

I remained the "lady of the villa" a little longer. I completed a couple of gorgeous paintings on the San Tropez marina. Then I was moved to a different position. Back then, people didn't believe what the newspapers reported as much. People became skeptical and suspicious. It began as early as my military service in the Air Force, as a radar operator. My job was to look at the radar and protect Israel's southern aerial border.

One day, as I worked the afternoon shift, I was sitting in front of the radar. Suddenly, I saw three new spots moving on the screen above the Egyptian border and into Israel territory. I then reported it to the Tel Aviv Command Center. Within a few seconds, the on-duty controller came into the radar trailer and so did the commanding officer. I continued to report datum points.

The controller took command of the situation.

According to the datum point speed, he noted that these were Egyptian MiGs. Israeli airplanes were immediately launched. One MiG turned around and flew back to Egypt, while the other two proceeded. One of our pilots flew in front of them, I think his name was Jack, or something like that. The other Israeli airplanes were still far away. The MiGs were close to the Israeli plane. The pilot was ordered: "Retreat!"

We heard the pilot's response: "I'm on his tail."

The controller replied: "Negative. Retreat, over."

We heard broken words and strange sounds. The pilot's voice was broken: "Can't hear... can't hear..." finally his voice cut out to radio silence.

Previously, there were three dots on the screen, the two MiGs and the Israeli pilot. Now, there was only one dot...

Our hearts skipped a beat. Suddenly, we heard the voice of the pilot again: "I took them both down!"

We all hugged. The controller was pleased. He was an amputee who'd lost his leg when his plane was hit by an Egyptian anti-aircraft missile. He was now overjoyed that he had taken part in shooting down the MiGs, as if he had finally gotten his revenge.

The commanding officer approached me and patted me on the shoulder. "Shosh, you did a great job," he said.

I felt good to be a part of it all.

In the evening, we all celebrated at the Hatzor Air Force base. Ezer Weizman, who was the commander of the Israeli Air Force back then, celebrated with us.

In the morning, I left home for a short time off. I walked to the train station. *Yediot Aharonot* and *Ma'ariv* headlines shouted in bold letters: "Israel Shot Down Two Egyptian MiGs." People simply couldn't believe it. They thought the media was making up stories to lift their spirits up. I wanted to cry out: "It's true. It really did happen!" But naturally, I couldn't do that.

On my way home, I bought some flowers for my mother. She'd prepared meatballs and a cheesecake for me to eat later. She kept a kosher home. In the past, she would go swimming, mostly at one of the quiet beaches by the Rambam hospital. People told me that she was one of the bravest swimmers and swam at least one and a half kilometers into the sea away from the shore. The quiet beach seldom had any waves, it was like a big lake. I couldn't understand how she wasn't afraid to swim that far.

When I was released from the army, I worked as a journalist for a couple of months and then I flew to France. I began working at the Israeli Tourism Bureau in Paris.

I had a lot of free time on my hands. I was contemplating whether I should learn Russian at the Sorbonne, or perhaps at the military school that had a Russian class. Finally, I chose the Sorbonne. I had no special reason for learning Russian at the time. I could have easily chosen Mandarin instead.

It's curious that the two most important men in my life were my late and loving husband, Alex, and my lover, Mike. Both of whom were of Russian origin, born in Riga, Latvia.

I signed up for a beginners and advanced course. Years later, I remembered very little of it as I lacked practice.

I met Jacques in Paris; he owned a fashion house. I broke up with him after I met Francois, who had finished medical school and specialized in otolaryngology. We dated for two years.

After having worked at the Tourism Bureau, I worked at the organizational department at the Jewish Agency and then the department of information. I worked at the East European Carmel Agrexco company, managed by kibbutz members. During the Algerian War, I worked at the European offices of Kol Israel radio with network administrator, Naftali Levin.

I learned art history at the Louvre school and focused mainly on impressionism.

I started working for different French papers and at a Jewish news magazine, *L'Arche*. The newspaper sent me to Geneva to participate at the global Jewish Congress led by the late Dr. Nahum Goldman. I sat next to the Italian delegate, a young woman from Milan who had just been engaged and wore an 8-carat diamond ring. When I got bored from the long speeches, my eyes wandered to the light bouncing off the ring's diamond. It's not every day that you get to see an 8-carat solitaire diamond. Perhaps only in the Cartier window displays on Rue De La Paix, or Van Cleef in Vendome square in Paris.

I remember Nahum Goldman's speech that came straight after an expert whose speech annoyed me. Dr. Nahum Goldman stood up and interrupted the expert's speech. "What is an expert after all?" he asked mockingly. "A man who knows one thing well, and nothing else!" he concluded.

I was still in Paris during the Six-Day War. I remember that during the occupation of the Western Wall from the Jordanians, we burst out screaming in joy and ran to pop open a bottle of champagne.

While in Paris, I loved to dine with my boyfriend, Francois, at L'Entrecote restaurant by Porte-Maillot, rather close to the Arc de Triomphe. People stood in line for their steak with its special sauce, cooked according to a unique eleven-ingredient recipe. No one could guess what the sauce truly contained. They had great chips, a fresh lettuce salad with a Dijon mustard dressing, and walnuts, and profiteroles for dessert.

Last year, I dined with Mike at the Peter Luger Steakhouse in New York (the Long Island branch), which was considered the best steak restaurant in the States. We ordered a main course to share – a huge steak. I asked that they cook it medium well. Mike asked for it to be well done. I said to him: "Let's order medium well first, and if it's too bloody, we'll ask them to make it well done. There's no going back from well done." Mike insisted it to be well done. Once again, Mike made sure he got his way.

The steak we were served was rather charred, but it was still the best steak I ever ate. The side dishes were wonderful spinach and fries. For dessert we had a rich strudel, topped with a mountain of fresh whipped cream. The meal was expensive, but we had a good time. It was worth it, and I would do it again, only this time, medium well. By the way, they don't accept credit cards in this restaurant. You can only pay with cash or the restaurant's credit card.

Then we returned to Mike's house. We had a sweet

and thick liqueur, something made in Ukraine, I can't quite remember its name.

I climbed up to the room and fell asleep. Mike went down to the basement and worked there for a couple of hours.

Finally, Mike came up to bed. I couldn't hear him coming in, but I felt him get into bed. I turned around and touched his shoulder. I wanted to feel his skin, his body. He responded with an overly dramatic sigh: "I'm tired."

I was offended. A man has never before told me that he was tired. And all I wanted was to touch him, to hold him. I was tired, too. 'Son of a bitch', I thought to myself. What came out of my mouth was just as vulgar.

"Fuck you!" I mumbled and turned around.

He said, "Shosh, you're rude!"

I had offended his highness. "Sorry!" I exclaimed.

What would our life together have looked like? Something along the lines of 'the wolf also shall dwell with the lamb, and the leopard shall lie down with the kid'?

I was reminded of the letters written by German poet, playwright and philosopher Johann Christoph Friedrich von Schiller: "Only those who love without hope know love!" In his play *Don Carlos* he says: "Great souls endure in silence."

I was reminded that my Alex had given his German prisoner of war an ancient poetry book by Friedrich Schiller. I remember Alex's kindness, who had made peace with all my whims. He never complained. I wish to touch him, caress and kiss him. But he lies deep in the ground, there in the Yarkon cemetery. Sometimes, I think of Sonya, Mike's late wife, who passed away from a violent illness. I cry with her. We are both victims of love.

The Flying Dutchman

The pleasant voyage on the luxury cruise ship from the Seychelles went on.

We sailed off the African coast and approached the Cape of Good Hope. It was a rocky cliff that emerged from the Atlantic Ocean waters in Southeastern Africa, about seventy kilometers from Cape Town, where we were supposed to dock. It was the meeting point of the Atlantic and Indian Oceans, a passageway between Europe and India. There was also Cape Agulhas, located one hundred and seventy kilometers from Cape Town, the most southern point in the African continent. This is the exact meeting point between the two oceans, the Indian and the Atlantic.

Before the construction of the Suez Canal, the capes were considered mysterious and dangerous for all sailors. Many lost their lives in that region due to strong currents, giant waves, blowing winds, storms and lightning. It was the epitome of wonder and the penultimate pain.

I tempted fate and went up to the deck at night. With such a big ship, our chances for a disaster were scant. And yet, there was an odd feeling to that cruise. I sat alone in a comfortable chair on the deck and covered myself with a raincoat. My hair was covered with a chic Hermes scarf, its ends blowing in the wind.

One cannot discuss the Cape of Good Hope without mentioning *The Flying Dutchman* and its damned crew. The night was pitch black. The moon was pale and light. Strong winds blew, carrying the souls of seamen who had perished in the previous centuries. I was reminded of the Flying Dutchman myth. Some say it is folklore about a ghost ship sailing the ocean forever, without being able to return home. One version claims the crew had a disease, which is why there weren't permitted to dock at any port. The ship and its crew were doomed to sail for eternity, never to return to shore. Another version, which seems closer to the truth, claims that the legend is based on Richard Wagner's opera. Wagner stated that he was inspired to write the opera when his ship was caught in a terrible storm on the Baltic Sea, sailing from Riga to London. The captain swore that he wouldn't shy away from a storm and would sail around the Cape of Good Hope, even if it meant his doom. According to the legend, no seaman's soul will rest until it is replaced with another.

I wonder how these "esteemed" Germans, listened in a "cultured" manner, with their bowties, to Richard Wagner – *The Valkyrie*; *The Flying Dutchman*; *Lohen-grin*; *Siegfried*; *Tannhäuser* – as their orders were carried out, and the Final Solution happened, the Holocaust in which millions of Jews were murdered. There is a horrific picture in the Yad Vashem archive, taken by a German soldier. In the picture, another German soldier is shooting a father as he holds his little son, with his pants around his ankles, close to his heart, while other "honorable" Germans, the initiators of the Final Solution, were listening to the wonderful music by the so-called anti-Semitic Wagner in a splendid hall.

Killing Me Softly

I didn't bother to make any friends on that cruise. If I would have stumbled across any interesting people, they would have noticed and approached me. I surrounded myself with a protective wall. I wallowed in missing Mike. Is this love? I felt that I had been breathing him for almost a year. The way I saw it, he had been my husband for two months! For a whole year I cried my eyes out whenever I thought of him. Did he feel it there, across the ocean? Was he thinking of me every day? Once a week? What does he feel for me? Did we share some form of telepathy? I didn't think so. Technically, it might be possible, but we don't know how to activate this kind of communication.

There were days I struggled to walk, even around the house. I think it was psychosomatic, something mental. I feel like my body is drained because it's away from Mike.

I feel like my immune system collapsing. I feel like he's sucking me dry, swallowing me whole, killing me softly. He was all the men I loved rolled into one. Why couldn't I simply forget him? Had everything we shared disappear? Was this all a Fata Morgana of love? I was thirsty for love, not water.

The dye had already been cast. I was on my way to him. He would wait for me at the Miami port. All I had to do was step off the ship and straight into his arms.

Once again, I am left alone to make my own decisions. What should I do?

As I write down these words and retrace everything that happened, it seems therapeutic. I couldn't forget him even if I wanted to. But despite it all, despite everything that has happened, my soul reaches out to him.

My daughter says: "Mom, why are you humiliating yourself? He doesn't want you. If he did, he would get on the first plane and come to you. Why can't you understand it?"

It's a magic circle, nothing comes in or goes out.

Once, I could move mountains. When I worked at the Agrexco company in Paris, they had an issue with a surplus of avocado. One Friday, before I left for my weekend vacation, I spoke to the company's CEO, a pleasant German kibbutznik from Ma'ayan Zvi. We spoke about the surplus of avocados and I asked why they didn't use the avocados for the cosmetics industry, or even for oil. He looked at me in astonishment. I explained to him that the cosmetics industry was also partially based on natural ingredients and women, for instance, slice cucumbers and use them as face masks. I think that eventually, I convinced him. The penny dropped.

At the entrance to their offices, there was an old guard who had a large and intimidating black dog, similar to the one in *The Hound of the Baskervilles*, who wasn't always on a leash. When I was a little girl, a dog had bit my buttocks as I was sitting on a fence which had a "beware of the dog" sign on it. I couldn't read back then, but the bite traumatized me. I was scared that I'd have to get fourteen Rabies shots in my tummy. I was haunted by these fears and would often be late to work because of that dog.

My kibbutznik bosses would rise early in the morning and were already at the office at 7 AM. I was supposed to arrive at 9 AM. Oh well, I tried. When I came back to work on Monday morning, the kibbutzniks waited for me in the office, and the CEO wouldn't even let me approach my workstation. In short, they fired me and gave me a golden parachute – double monthly payments, vacations, days off, and so on. After some time, I heard from a friend who had replaced me, that they did tests in important French labs to check if the avocados were indeed suitable for the cosmetics industry. In the meantime, there was a new Israeli CEO. And the rest is history.

Even though I thought I had been mistreated, and they should have shared the development of the idea with me, I was proud that I had indeed done something. Without me or my idea, the avocado would not have been a part of the cosmetics industry. At least not at that stage.

How to Lead a Horse to Water

The ship had already sailed over the waters of the Atlantic Ocean. Soon, after a few stops at the nearby islands, we would arrive at Miami. I would no longer have breakfasts in front of the ocean turquoise shades, the white foam of the waves and the occasionally flying fish. I also had the privilege of seeing a whale fin rise above the waves in all its glory.

I was far from home. Far from my daughter and my grandchildren. Who would I miss more? Bliss is never perfect. There would always be a hint of imperfection, something that remains incomplete. What can I do in my age except for work out, eat and make love? I can go to the hair salon, get a mani-pedi and be beautiful for Mike; I can buy gifts for my grandchildren and sit with friends at a café as we gossip about everyone; I can buy different brands; sometimes go to the synagogue, light

Friday candles and cook a meal for Shabbat; I can try to be healthy and not be a burden to those around me. I don't want Mike thinking he is my caregiver. All the options looked rather boring. Was there something else that would satisfy me?

Here I was on the deck, facing an infinite blue ocean and incessantly complaining about my ill fate. I could have chosen a less romantic backdrop for that. I'm on my way to Mike, the man I love. Who needs anything more?

The ship arrived in Miami and was tied to the dock. I walked onto the deck in a thin cotton dress, my hair blowing in the wind. I saw Mike standing on the dock, with his perennial beret. My heart skipped a beat.

The passengers stepped off. I went to talk with the purser.

"The ship continues its voyage to the Easter Islands after passengers disembark," he said.

I told him I was staying onboard and asked that he let me know when the ship was leaving. He promised to do so.

I went back to my cabin. Why didn't I get off? Why did I leave Mike at the dock?

Those questions remain unanswered.

I poured myself a glass of Merlot. The sun's rays shone into the cabin. A pleasant breeze blew across the ocean.

I heard the swift sounds of angel wings.

There was a knock on the door. 'That must be the purser, coming to tell me about the rest of the voyage,' I thought.

I opened the door.

Much to my surprise, it was Mike at the door, with an apologetic smile and a bag in his hand. He handed it to me and said: "It's not a million dollars, just fifty thousand. Is it enough to buy me a hug?"

He grabbed me in his arms and embraced me tightly. We both cried and he said: "**If the mountain won't come to Muhammad, then Muhammad must go to the mountain!**"

Printed in the USA
CPSIA information can be obtained
at www.ICGtesting.com
LVHW020417061023
760257LV00002B/38